LINEAR TACTICAL SERIES

SCOUT

D1509638

USA TODAY BESTSELLING AUTHOR

JANIE CROUCH

SCOUT: LINEAR TACTICAL

To Marci…
This book exists because of your perseverance and insistence that Nadine get her HEA. 🩶
Proof that we should never stop fighting for what we want.

Chapter 1

Wyatt Highfield had drawn the short straw more than once when it came to shitty situations.

It had been a regular part of life during his decade in the Special Forces. Drawing the short straw once in the Kunar Province of Afghanistan, he'd been the first to enter a Taliban hideout that had been reportedly empty. It had almost cost him his life. The bullet meant for his head had fortunately gone wide and only hit him in the shoulder.

Another short straw? He'd once spent six hours crammed inside a metal box, ready to be backup for his teammates during an off-book op in Venezuela involving a hijacked plane. He'd been fairly certain he'd never stretch back out to his full six foot four again after that.

His Special Forces days were behind him, but he'd drawn the short straw again. Today shouldn't have been nearly as traumatic as his other short-straw drawings.

"There he is. There is my good friend, Wyatt Highfield!"

But it was. Maybe the *most* traumatic.

Wyatt was sitting in a diner of questionable quality on the outskirts of Salt Lake City. The short straw this time meant agreeing to meet with Frank Jenkins, the current loud-mouth walking toward Wyatt and announcing to everyone and their mothers who Wyatt was.

"Jenkins. Good to see you." Wyatt stood up to shake the younger man's hand, his mother's etiquette instructions still ingrained into his DNA all these years later.

And if *good to see you* was a white lie, well then . . .

"Good to see you too, man! Just looking at your face makes me miss Oak Creek and all our buddies on the Linear Tactical team."

Wyatt barely refrained from rolling his eyes. None of the guys would truly consider Frank to be a friend or part of the team. But the man had once done what he could to save Anne Mackay's life, so all the guys at Linear Tactical were willing to cut the kid some slack.

"How's Salt Lake City been treating you?" Wyatt asked. "And your girlfriend? What was her name? Cindy?"

Frank had left Oak Creek about a year ago to follow some nurse he'd fallen in love with and planned to marry.

"Oh man, Cindy is old news. We broke up like six months ago."

Oh shit. The guys should be thanking their lucky stars Frank hadn't moved back and continued his attempt to join the ranks of Linear Tactical. He'd wanted to for years, although he had neither the training, discipline, nor mindset.

If it were just the training Frank lacked, Wyatt and the guys probably would've helped and encouraged him until he was ready to join their survival, self-defense, and weapons training business.

But the lack of discipline and an incorrect mindset weren't things they messed around with. Someone who wanted to be a part of Linear Tactical solely to prove how tough they were and to play with weapons was not a good fit. Frank probably wouldn't ever be ready.

"I'm sorry to hear about your breakup."

The waitress brought Frank coffee without him asking for it. The man must be in here pretty regularly.

"Naw, man. It's all good. I got a new girlfriend. Destiny." Frank leaned closer, but his voice was just as loud. "She's a stripper. Want to see a picture?"

Oh sweet Jesus, no. There was no telling what state of undress Frank would be willing to show in a picture of his girlfriend. "No thanks. I'm good."

"She works down the street."

And that explained Frank's familiarity with the diner. "Okay."

"You don't want to see a picture because of Nadine, right?" Frank winked at him, and Wyatt's teeth ground together. He took a sip of his truly horrible coffee.

It was one thing for his friends and former Special Forces teammates—men who'd held his life in their hands, and vice versa—to poke at him about his relationship with Nadine. Frank Jenkins was not one of those people.

"You guys dating yet, or what?"

Don't punch him in the face. Don't punch him in the face.

Wyatt wasn't about to elaborate on Nadine, especially with Frank, who only knew about the situation because he made it his business to collect as much gossip about the Linear guys as he could—Frank's way of making himself relevant. Since the Nadine situation had occurred before he'd left Oak Creek, Frank was relatively well versed.

Another sip of coffee. "No. Not yet."

"Right on, brother. You got to bide your time when it comes to the ladies." Frank actually held his fist out to be bumped.

"Something like that." Wyatt held his cup up toward the waitress for a refill rather than give Frank the approval he sought for his obnoxious comment.

Because the situation with Nadine wasn't Wyatt biding his time to make a play for someone he had a crush on.

Or wasn't *only* that.

Nadine MacFarlane still needed time to heal from her wounds—physical and emotional— even though it had been more than two years. That sort of recovery took as long as it took. Couldn't be rushed. And he definitely wouldn't be rushing her.

Although, as soon as she showed signs of being ready to reenter the normal world, Wyatt would be the first one at her door.

After all, they'd been electronic pen pals for more than two years now. As soon as she showed any interest at all, he was ready to take their friendship to the next level.

So yeah, maybe he'd said no to Zac Mackay when the man had offered to come meet Frank, since it was Zac who owed him the most for saving Anne's life. And yeah, that might have to do with the fact that to get to Salt Lake City on the five-hour drive from Oak Creek, he had to drive near McCammon, Idaho.

And yeah, that happened to be where Nadine MacFarlane lived.

None of this he planned on telling Frank.

It was time to get to the point. "Okay, Jenkins. Why are we here? Something about a computer drive?"

"Oh yeah, right." He sounded like he'd actually forgotten about his frantic call a couple days ago. His insistence that the drive could not be mailed. That it had to be delivered in person to someone from Linear Tactical.

Frank took another sip of coffee, as if he needed to be any more caffeinated. "So I was out late with the boys the other night before going to see Destiny. We were at this grocery store that has a little snack bar area, and we were getting pizza. They have pretty decent pizza for a place like that. You would think—"

"Frank. Focus. The drive."

"Right. Right. Anyway, my friend Keith was talking about how he wanted to apply for a job with Zodiac Tactical. Evidently, they might be opening up some jobs in Vegas and are looking for people to fit the bill."

Frank and his friends had as much chance of getting a job with Zodiac Tactical as they did with Linear. Wyatt knew the owner, Ian DeRose, personally, and the man did not tolerate less than the very best in his company. "Okay."

"Anywho, I mentioned to my friend Keith that I knew Ian DeRose."

Wyatt raised an eyebrow. "Do you know Ian?"

Frank huddled down into the booth a little more. "No. But I know Gabe Collingwood. They were SEALs together, and Gabe and I are relatively tight."

Somehow, Wyatt didn't think Gabe would see it that way. But he and Frank were going to be here all night if he didn't keep Frank on task. "Okay, drive?"

"Yeah, well, there was this old guy at the grocery store. He followed me out to the parking lot—scared the shit out of me—and asked if I could get him in touch with Ian DeRose."

Okay, vaguely interesting. "What did he want with Ian?"

"Said he had a computer drive he needed to get to Ian or someone connected to him."

"Why didn't the guy just walk into one of Zodiac's dozen offices and hand it over? Ian might not have met with the guy personally, but he would've at least looked into it."

"Dude was really nervous. Checking over his shoulder every couple seconds. He said that he needed to get the drive somewhere safe but couldn't use any computers or telephones."

Wyatt scrubbed a hand down his face. This was starting to sound like one of those *Mission: Impossible* movies. "Okay, start over. What was this guy's name?"

Frank looked a little sheepish. "Claude Seventy or something. I'm not great with names."

"Claude Seventy." That could not possibly be right. "Let's call him Claude. Claude heard you mention Ian and approached you."

"Yup."

"And Claude felt like he couldn't contact any of the Zodiac offices himself because it was too dangerous."

Frank nodded multiple times. "Exactly. Said he was being monitored."

"So you told Claude that you would hand over the drive to your good friend Ian DeRose?" Wyatt raised an eyebrow.

"Actually, I admitted I didn't really know Ian. That's where you guys come in. I told Claude about Linear Tactical and how you guys are basically heroes and that I could get the drive to you guys and you could probably get it to Ian or whatever."

Wyatt swallowed another sip of the horrible coffee, trying to force himself to remain patient. To not get up and walk out even though with every sentence this was looking more and more like a waste of time. "You know we're not a delivery service, right?"

Frank was finally tuning in to Wyatt's annoyance. "Yeah, of course, man. I know. Old Man Claude said the drive contained info about an organization that was doing a lot of bad stuff. That he was trying to stop them from growing a human trafficking ring."

Human trafficking. Wyatt sat up straighter. "What organization?"

"I don't know. Claude didn't tell me."

"Do you have a way of getting in touch with Claude?"

"No. He got spooked by something and took off. But he gave me this." Frank pulled a small computer drive out of his jacket pocket and slid it across to Wyatt. "He said everything's on here. Told me to get it to my friends. I told him about Kendrick and how he's a wiz with computers."

Wyatt studied the drive, not at all surprised that Frank had run his mouth about everyone he knew. That was how the kid rolled.

Wyatt was glad to see the device Frank gave him was actually an external computer drive, and a very high-end one at that—not something you'd pick up at the local computer superstore. It even seemed to have its own mini power source of some sort. When Wyatt flipped on the small switch, an LED flashed every few seconds. He flipped the switch off.

Wyatt was highly skeptical that this thing held anything of much value, but he would take it and give it to Kendrick. And make sure Kendrick knew to run it for any possible computer viruses before opening it—not that the other man ever needed to be reminded of anything when it came to computers.

"All right, Frank. I'll take it back to Kendrick, and we'll go from there. If Ian and Zodiac Tactical need to be brought in on it, we'll do so."

"Thanks, man. The old guy was way serious about this thing. And if it does have to do with some organization involved with human trafficking, it would be awesome if our team could stop it."

Our team. Sigh.

Wyatt ran through all the details one more time with Frank to make sure there wasn't anything more he could dig out of the man's brain, but unsurprisingly, the man's story had all the same holes. Wyatt signaled to the waitress and paid for both his and Frank's coffee, leaving a generous tip.

She probably needed it if she had to put up with Frank on a regular basis.

He slid out of the booth. "You did the right thing by calling, Frank. If this Claude guy contacts you again, be sure to get his full name. Have him write it down for you. Or better still, get his number so we can contact him."

He and Frank walked out of the diner. Darkness had fallen over the city as they hit the parking lot.

"I'll be in touch, Frank." He turned to walk toward his car.

"Hey, Wyatt, before you go . . ." Frank jogged to keep up. "Do you think you could come by Panthers with me? That's where Destiny works. She and I kind of got in a fight last week."

"I think you better patch that one up yourself."

Frank gave an awkward laugh. "Well, I sort of got drunk with the fellas last night and left a bunch of messages on her voice mail. Told her all about the drive and you guys and how Kendrick was going to crack it and we were going to shut down a human trafficking ring. Told her I might be going to Oak Creek to help."

Wyatt stopped. "So, you basically told her you were going to be a hero."

Frank shrugged and made an almost comical face. "Yeah. Pretty much exactly."

Not a single word about that surprised Wyatt. He started walking toward his car again.

"I was hoping you could pop in to Panthers, introduce yourself so Destiny knows Linear Tactical is real, and casually mention that I gave you the drive so you could stop some really bad guys."

Right. Because that would all come up so casually in conversation. Maybe while she was giving him a lap dance.

"I tell you what, Frank. If this drive does hold info that

takes down some *really bad guys*, I will personally bring the entire Linear Tactical team to Panthers to sing your praises in front of your lady friend. We will make sure she knows you're a true hero—"

Wyatt heard the sound of gunfire at the same moment Frank's head exploded right in front of him and the man crumpled to the ground.

Dead.

Years of training took over, and Wyatt dropped to the ground in an instant, pulling out his weapon from his ankle holster as he went. Not half a second later, a bullet nailed the car where he'd been standing.

Right next to Frank's dead body.

God fucking damn it.

"I'm so, so sorry, kid." Wyatt reached over and squeezed Frank's ankle before scurrying away, crawling under cars in the opposite direction from where the gun had fired. More shots came at him.

Someone screamed from the doorway of the diner and pandemonium erupted. Wyatt crouched behind a car, ready to return fire if the person who'd killed Frank decided to go for anyone else in the crowd forming outside. But there was nothing.

Whoever had been shooting had specifically targeted Frank and Wyatt. And now Frank was dead.

Whatever the hell was on that drive had just become a shit ton more dangerous.

Chapter 2

"I'm not a recluse, Chloe."

On the other end of the call, Nadine MacFarlane heard the snicker that her best friend made no attempt to muffle.

"Seriously, I'm not."

"Hang on," Chloe said. "I'm looking up recluse in the dictionary right now and . . . yep, that's what I thought. There's a picture of *you* next to the word."

Nadine loved Chloe Jeffries Westman like a sister. She truly did. Growing up in foster care together had given them that closeness. But right now, Chloe was being a pain in the ass.

"Dictionaries don't have pictures," Nadine muttered, lying back on her small couch and looking out the window. "Besides, my job lets me work from home, so why wouldn't I stay here? I like it here."

Chloe let out a long-suffering sigh. "How about for some interaction? With actual people, not on the computer. *Getting out of the house* kind of interaction."

"I leave my house."

"Going to the farmer's market once a week or hiking by yourself does not count as leaving the house."

Nadine grimaced, glad they weren't video chatting so Chloe couldn't see how right on target she was. "I go other places."

"Oh yeah? Where?"

It wasn't the first time they'd had this conversation, and Nadine had the feeling it wouldn't be the last. Chloe worried about her.

She had reason to. And they both knew it.

Nadine let out a sigh. "It's not like I don't try, Chlo. I honestly do. I'm not interested in being around people."

"Which is the definition of a recluse—"

"Hush, woman. Where's your sexy husband and adorable toddler? Can't you go bother them? Or isn't there anything with the show that needs your attention?"

Chloe was the creative director of *Day's End*, one of the most successful programs on television for six years running. Nadine had once been a part of that too.

Chloe laughed. "Shane is at a security meeting for the show. You know him, takes my safety so seriously. Even though there hasn't been any danger since . . ." She trailed off.

She didn't need to say it—they both knew what she was talking about. Chloe had almost died thanks to Nadine's shitty choices in men.

And Nadine still bore the scars in every way someone could bear them.

"I love you, Nay-Nay. But it's been more than two years. Nobody blames you for what—"

"I know." Nobody blamed her except herself. "I'm not ready to jump back into the world. I'm taking it slow."

"You know there's always room back here in North

Carolina. You should at least come for a visit. It's been too long."

Nadine's move to Idaho—not only Idaho, but McCammon, Idaho, one of the least populated towns in one of the least populated states—had changed the daily dynamics of their friendship.

"I know. I want to. I miss you." But returning to North Carolina was still too hard. Too entwined with the pain she was trying to forget. Idaho was better, safer.

Idaho didn't stop her from waking up at night, screaming and trapped in a nightmare, trying to douse the phantom agony of her burning flesh. But at least she didn't have to talk to anyone the next day about what had happened.

She didn't have to talk to anyone at all.

"Plus . . ." Nadine could hear the smile in Chloe's voice. "I could definitely use an assistant here. I had one a few years ago who spoiled me for everyone who's come after. There's no replacing her."

Nadine snatched her hand away from the burn scars that covered both her legs up to midthigh. It was sick the way her fingers sometimes trailed the pattern. She sat up on the couch. "If you hadn't recommended me to so many of your Hollywood acquaintances as a virtual assistant, you'd probably have an easier time luring me back. I have so much work, I have to turn away clients."

"I'm glad work is good and fulfilling for you, but it's not enough, and you know it. Go out to a restaurant. Or have a drink at a bar. Someplace where you can talk to people face-to-face. Talk to a *man* face-to-face."

What exactly would she say? *Nice to meet you. I'm the idiot who didn't realize my last boyfriend was a psychopath intent on killing my best friend.*

Suppose she could find someone she could trust. The thought of having to eventually tell him about what had happened made her physically ill. And it wasn't as if she could keep it a secret. The incident and all its fallout had made national headlines.

Not to mention, one look at her legs told a pretty damned big story of its own. An ugly one.

"I don't have time for a man, Chlo. Being a virtual assistant takes as much time every day as being your assistant ever did, but over the computer."

Chloe's voice got softer. "This isn't about making room in your schedule for a man. This is about being willing to open yourself up. About having balance."

"My life has balance. I would rather be home is all. Or hiking or walking in the woods. I even kayak. That's a healthy activity, right? I get outside. I get plenty of fresh air and sunshine."

"Alone."

"I like it that way." Nobody stared at her when she was alone. The trees and little animals never gaped at her legs. She didn't have to wear long pants on hot days the way she would if she had to be around people.

"Nadine." Chloe's voice dropped in pitch. Nadine had known her friend long enough to know that meant a lecture was coming. "Nobody wants to rush you in your recovery. But it's been more than two years since . . . the incident."

Nadine stood up and walked over to the window. Part of the reason she'd moved to Idaho last year was because it was becoming harder to hide that she was getting worse, not better, when it came to her recovery. The less she was around people, the harder it was to be around them at all.

"I know, Chlo."

"There has to come a time when you start living again. I don't want you to be lonely."

"I'm not lonely. I talk to people every day. It just happens to be via computer. I'm almost always talking to somebody."

"Like Wyatt Highfield? Are you still talking to him?"

Nadine straightened at the window, eyes narrowing. Chloe could be so sly when she wanted to be. This was probably what the entire call was about. "We email or message each other a few times a week. Or sometimes we call each other."

And it was always the highlight of Nadine's week, but she wasn't about to tell Chloe that. Little Miss Matchmaker would pounce.

"Well, you know what Shane thinks about him." Chloe's husband had served in the Special Forces with Wyatt for nearly ten years. "Says he's a good guy. In Shane-speak, that's a huge compliment."

"I'm sure it is. And I don't doubt Wyatt is a good guy. But, you know . . . he was there. He saw me at my lowest, my most stupid. There's no way he'd want to ever be more than friends." Nadine winced as silence thundered through the phone connection. She had no doubt this was merely the calm before the—

"Nadine MacFarlane, you're lucky you're in BF, Idaho so I can't slap you upside the head. I cannot believe you could say something so fucking stupid about your—" Chloe's words got louder and faster as she went along.

"Uh-oh. Go put a dollar in the curse jar. I hope my goddaughter isn't around."

Chloe spoke right over her. "You're a good person who got taken advantage of by an asshole. It happens. That doesn't mean you were stupid. Travis wasn't worthy of the ground you walk on, and he's sure as hell not worth your emotional energy two years later."

Nadine appreciated her friend's support—unwavering as it had been since they were kids. But she knew the truth.

If you were smart, you didn't think someone was in love

with you when they were only using you. Not just using you, but willing to leave you to die horribly.

And once you realized how incredibly stupid you were for having trusted your instincts about someone, how could you ever possibly trust those instincts again?

"Regardless," Chloe continued, "Wyatt is nothing like Travis."

"I'm sure you're right."

"You should give him a chance."

"A chance to do what? We're the modern-day equivalent of pen pals. We've joked about it. He's not interested in anything more."

"Did he say that, or did you deduce it for yourself?"

"Come on, Chloe, you've seen the man. He's gorgeous."

And friendly and smart and . . . fun. She always looked forward to chatting with Wyatt online. He made her feel comfortable, joked, and . . . flirted a little.

Or, at least, she thought it was flirting. "He's never mentioned meeting in person, so obviously that's not what he wants. He's a buddy."

And perhaps the only man in the world Nadine would consider going out with.

But she'd never hear the end of it if she ever shared that with Chloe. Her friend would start planning the wedding before they got off the phone. She'd have her husband, Shane, call all the Linear Tactical guys to put pressure on Wyatt to ask her out.

That was the last thing Nadine wanted. A pity date. Especially from Wyatt. So she'd keep him as her pen-pal-buddy-friend.

And continue to be the most pathetic creature on the planet.

Chloe let out a huge sigh. "He might want to be more than your buddy. It wouldn't kill you to ask more personal questions. Find out if he wants to get together for real. *In person*. Where kissing and canoodling might happen."

That brought out a smile. "*Canoodling?* Really, Chlo?"

"Would you prefer I say, 'get naked and have hot sex on the kitchen table'?"

She looked over at her table. It wasn't very large, but it was solid wood. Images of Wyatt's big, strong body covering hers on it flooded her mind.

He was big enough to make her—five foot ten and definitely not small boned—feel feminine and girly. The picture of him spreading her out on the table and crawling on top of her—

"No," she choked out. "Canoodling is fine."

Face—and other parts of her body—flaming, she left the kitchen and walked into her bedroom. It was Monday afternoon, which meant it was time for her weekly trip to the Fresh Market. Yes, her only regular outing from the house to converse face-to-face with others.

Being around people wasn't easy. But delicious produce and fresh flowers were worth dragging out her rusty interpersonal skills. Surrounding herself with fresh and pretty soothed her soul.

"There won't ever be any canoodling if you don't express interest," Chloe continued. "You need to go out with him!"

"He doesn't even know where I live. We haven't seen each other in person since . . ." Since she'd been lying helpless in the hospital. Dislocated wrist, broken nose, cracked ribs, agonizing burns all over her legs. Wanting to die, but trying to give Shane and Wyatt any information she could to help find Chloe.

"Of course Wyatt knows where you live."

"No he doesn't. He's never asked."

"I know for a fact he knows. After all, he's friends with

Shane, isn't he? And he works for Linear Tactical. They make it their job to know stuff."

Nadine rolled her eyes and glanced at her long brown hair in the mirror, tucked up in its messy bun, as usual. No need to fix it or add makeup to her face to go to the market. She wouldn't be seeing anyone who cared.

"I'll tell you what. If Wyatt ever mentions anything about us getting together for a date, I'll accept. But you know his work for Linear Tactical takes him all over the place. Not exactly conducive to dating."

"All I'm asking is that you don't shut yourself off to the idea. It's time to get back in the game."

Nadine rubbed her fingers across her forehead. "I'm open to it. Okay? Is that enough?"

"Sigh. I guess so. Just talk to him the next time you have a chance. See if there's something there between you two."

"*Sigh*," Nadine mimicked. "Fine."

Chloe laughed, and they said their goodbyes. Nadine changed into a loose, flowy blouse and jeans. Being around people was easier when her legs were covered, and the mild weather today would allow for that.

Flowers would cheer the place up a little. Not that her little house wasn't comfortable and cute, but fresh flowers on her desk and next to her bed always made her feel good. They made working long hours easier to deal with too.

Although fresh flowers wouldn't make her any less lonely, would they?

Damn Chloe. Making her question things she would rather not spend time thinking about at all.

She wasn't lonely; she was alone. There was a difference. This was her choice. It was the way she liked it.

Damn it.

She pushed all those thoughts away as she drove to the market and wandered from one vendor to another. There was so much lush, colorful produce to choose from. The scent of so many different flowers to breathe in.

This made her happy. This was enough.

Or . . . at least, she could fool herself into believing it was for a little while.

The tote bags pulling at her shoulders were full an hour into the trip, and she still hadn't picked up flowers. She headed to the booth that had become her favorite and grinned when the vendor recognized her.

"I think I'll go with a dozen of the pink roses and two dozen daisies." A little extravagant, but she was going to treat herself. She handed cash to the vendor.

"Roses and daisies. That's an unusual combination." The man's voice was muffled behind her as she grabbed the large bouquets from the vendor.

"I don't plan on putting them together."

"Are you sure? Sometimes the most unlikely pair makes the most striking combination."

She stiffened and turned, unable to process what she was hearing. *Who* she was hearing. But that deep baritone was unmistakable.

As were the ruggedly handsome face and broad shoulders she found as she completed her turn.

As if her conversation with Chloe had conjured him, Wyatt Highfield was here.

Chapter 3

"*Wyatt?*"

When Wyatt had hoped to stop by and see Nadine on his way back from Salt Lake City, this had very definitely not been what he'd had in mind. He'd given many hours of thought to how their first face-to-face meeting in years should go.

Lying and using her to get out of a desperate situation was not it.

There were literally traces of blood on his hands, which he thrust into his pockets at the sight of Nadine's surprised smile as she stood in front of him, arms full with bags of fruit and flowers.

And looking downright delicious. Not that he ever didn't find her delicious.

He should not have come here.

He gave her what he hoped was a charming smile, hiding the aches from the bruises that covered his torso and arms after having his car run off the road. Thankfully, none were on his face, which would have immediately led to questions.

Not that him being here at the Fresh Market didn't bring up enough questions on its own.

It had been a shitty three days from the moment Frank had been murdered in front of him. He'd been on the run from the beginning—barely making it out of the parking lot before the cops had arrived.

He'd wanted to stay and give his account to the police, but if someone was willing to kill Frank for that drive, they'd do the same to Wyatt. Whatever was on that piece of equipment was pretty fucking important.

So he'd run. He'd had to leave his car in the parking lot at the diner, which had required keeping his head down and walking a few miles until he got to a rundown motel, where he'd thought he'd be safe to wait for an extraction from the Linear guys.

The killers had found him before he'd been able to place the call. It was only because he'd gotten a room with both a front and back door that he wasn't dead right now.

He'd immediately ditched his phone. Frank had run his mouth about Linear, so probably all their cells were compromised. Contacting his friends directly wasn't an option.

He'd stolen a car to get the hell out of the city. But no matter what he did—and this wasn't Wyatt's first time using evasive driving techniques—the bad guys kept finding him. He'd lose one tail only to have another on him a half hour later.

These people were obviously not only deadly, but also well connected. They had access to cameras and security feeds to track him.

That meant getting off the highway and hoping they didn't have satellite access. But they still had something because they'd been back on his ass a few hours later, despite stopping, switching vehicles, and driving in every haphazard direction possible.

A shootout about ten miles south of here before the sun came up this morning had left two dead bad guys, Wyatt covered in bruises, and his stolen car out of action in a ditch where they'd run him off the road.

The killers would be looking for him again soon, but they'd assume he would head toward Idaho Falls. A big city would be the best chance for Wyatt to hide in a crowd.

Instead, he'd gone the opposite direction. Toward the tiny town of McCammon.

Toward Nadine.

He'd been awake for more than forty-eight hours. He needed somewhere to lie low—a place to find shelter for a few hours while he figured out what the hell he was going to do. He needed to get this drive to Kendrick at Linear Tactical, but he couldn't take a chance on contacting them directly.

He'd dashed into the town's superstore and bought a pay-as-you-go cell phone with nearly the last of his cash. He'd needed to get it somewhere where it could charge. He'd stepped out of the store and seen the market.

The one place she said she went every week. He'd been unable to resist turning in that direction.

But he shouldn't have come here. Shouldn't have given in to this need to see her with his own eyes. Even if he needed it in a way he didn't understand.

"Oh, wow, Nadine. What a surprise!" Everything in him rebelled at the lies he told. "I can't believe it. Isn't it a small world?"

"Wh-what are you doing here?" Her hazel eyes were big. The hands holding the flowers started to tremble. "Oh my God. Please, please tell me you didn't talk to Chloe."

"Chloe Westman? Shane's wife?" He didn't have to pretend any confusion about this. "Should I have talked to her about something?"

"Never mind." Her cheeks flushed before she turned back to the flower vendor to finish their transaction.

Wyatt's eyes darted around the area. He didn't see anyone. But if the guys chasing him had found him again, they'd be searching for one man by himself, not a couple shopping together.

He should walk away. Should never have come into this market to begin with. But he'd known she was here, known this was the only place she went every week, and couldn't force himself to stay away.

He was a grade-A bastard.

"I can't believe you're here." She turned back to him, genuine gladness in her smile.

Exactly what he'd always hoped he'd see when they finally met again face-to-face.

Grade-A bastard.

"Crazy, isn't it? Do you mind if I walk with you for a few minutes?"

"Sure. That would be really nice." She rubbed her cheek along the soft petals of the roses wrapped in paper. He didn't think it was possible to be jealous of a plant, but damn, how many times had he wished he could touch her skin, even in the most innocent of ways?

How many times had he touched a screen over the past couple of years while reading her words, or looking at a picture she'd sent him, hoping someday she'd let him trail his fingers against her hand? Her cheek. More.

The guys would've laughed their asses off if they could've seen it. But Wyatt hadn't cared.

"Can I carry something? It looks like you've got your hands full."

"Thanks." She handed him one of her canvas bags full of food and the bunch of daisies, keeping the second bag and roses for herself. "Um, are you in town on business?"

"I'm here for a . . . meeting, but my car broke down." Neither were technically lies, if you were willing to call his tires and windshield being shot out *broken down*. "I'm waiting for my replacement vehicle, so I figured I would walk around the market for a little while."

She stared at him for a moment. "You really didn't talk to Chloe? It's okay to tell me if you did. I won't tell her. I know she's scary."

He didn't tend to think of Shane's petite wife as scary, but she was definitely protective of Nadine. And yes, he did know her. Talked to her every once in a while due to that protectiveness.

Another something he really didn't want to bring up right now since it also might send Nadine running for the hills.

"I haven't talked to Chloe recently, I promise." Again, the truth. Despite everything, he wanted to lie to her as little as possible. "Why do you keep wondering about that?"

"I . . . She . . . We were . . ." She closed her eyes and shook her head. "Forget it. How have you been? We haven't talked much this week."

Her face was as pink as the roses in her arms, and he wanted nothing more than to coax her into telling him what was causing the blush—obviously, something having to do with Chloe. But he left it alone. They began strolling down the aisle.

"I've been busy." The understatement of the century. "I've missed being able to talk to you the past few days. Have you been okay?"

He leaned a little closer to breathe in her scent as she looked down at some vegetables on a table. Just doing so made him feel steadier. It didn't wash away the sight of Frank dying right in front of him or running for his life since, but at least he had the reminder that for every evil in this world, there was someone like Nadine. Good, kind, innocent.

She glanced back at him with another shy smile. "Yeah, I'm okay. Lots of work—the usual. But otherwise, mostly quiet."

"Quiet sounds really nice." More than nice. He'd give anything for a few hours of quiet.

They walked to the next booth. "Yeah, your life is so filled with excitement. I'm sometimes surprised you have time to talk to me."

"I find the time for people who matter." That, at least, wasn't a lie. Their little online courtship was the sweetest, nicest thing in his life.

And courtship was exactly the right word for it, at least for him. The way to give her all the time she needed to heal, but still be a part of her life.

But now he needed to leave her alone again.

Her mouth made the most adorable little O, and all he wanted to do was kiss the delighted surprise right off her lips.

But it would have to wait for another time when he wasn't in the middle of a critical mission.

He glanced down at his watch. "Damn it, I've got to be getting back to my meeting."

The delight slid out of her features. "Right, of course."

"But I'm really glad I got to see you." He felt like he'd kicked a puppy into oncoming traffic. "I'll call you next week, and we'll talk." Getting away from her was the right thing to do, but it was fucking hard.

"Okay."

"Are you done here? Can I walk you out to your car?" He gave her the friendliest smile he could manage, wishing he could do much more.

"Sure."

They turned toward the direction of the main exit, and Wyatt froze. Standing there were two men, scouring the crowd.

The killers had found him again.

Chapter 4

Wyatt turned back toward Nadine, calling himself every foul name he'd ever heard during his years in the army—plus a few more creative ones.

"You know what? Forget meetings and work. I'd rather stay here with you." He grabbed the bag and flowers from her again, keeping the flowers near his face to make it more difficult to see him from the side. "Do you have a little time?"

She gave a surprised little laugh. "Sure. I love it here."

She started walking back in the same direction they'd been going, but he turned her toward the next aisle instead, away from the encroaching danger.

He fell in step beside her, moving from one booth to another. Out of the corner of his eye, he caught Guy One. He'd split off from his partner, each looking for him separately.

The fact that they were looking for a single man rather than a couple was Wyatt's saving grace. He stepped closer to strengthen that ruse and felt like shit when she gave him a shy smile.

God, he wanted that smile. Just didn't want it under these circumstances.

As Guy Two cut way too close, Wyatt grabbed Nadine's arm gently, trailing his fingers along the skin at her elbow like he'd been wanting to for over two damned years and pointed to a batch of flowers in a large bucket on the ground. They both bent down to look at it.

"These are lilies right? Miniature ones?" he asked.

"They're actually called alstroemerias. But yes, they're a type of mini lily, and they last a long time in a vase. They're some of my favorites."

"You'll have to get those next time."

Guy Two passed behind them, and Wyatt stood back up, his fingers still on her arm. That wasn't necessary for subterfuge; he just wanted the touch of her skin under his hand as long as possible.

"So, what did you buy today?" He took note of the main exit to the south. There was another exit directly behind them, then one positioned in the center of a long row of booths. All of them emptied onto busy streets, which didn't work in his favor since he had no vehicle.

Nadine strolled alongside him, pointing out her favorite booths and what she usually liked to buy there.

"You look tired. Is that rude of me to say?" she said out of the blue as they continued strolling down an aisle.

"Not rude, honest." He scrubbed a hand down his face. "I am tired."

And feeling worse with every second he put her in danger. He needed to use her to get away from here. Maybe he could ask to borrow her car. She had no ties to Linear Tactical. The bad guys would have no reason to be looking for her at all.

Good. Nadine was the last person he wanted to pull into danger. She'd already been through enough.

He knew her wounds ran deeper than the burn scars on her legs. There was a reason she never went anywhere, why she essentially secluded herself after all this time. They'd never talked about it directly in all their online chats, but he knew the fear that drove her.

They chatted some more as they walked, sidestepping a group of kids who were ordering insanely overloaded crepes. The aroma made his mouth water. When was the last time he'd eaten more than a handful of whatever he could find at the nearest gas station convenience store?

"I've got to say, they're making me hungry." He nodded toward the crepe booth.

"I'm a sucker for the fresh scones myself," Nadine admitted. "They're so rich and buttery. I always get some. I look forward to them all week long."

He was about to admit he'd never eaten a scone in his life when the appearance of Guy One and Guy Two conversing at the end of the aisle had him slipping an arm around her. They hadn't seen him but would if they looked in this direction.

"I'm sold. Let's get a scone." He took Nadine by the elbow and hustled her between booths in the opposite direction from the men. "Where can I find them?"

She laughed. "Hang on a second! I'm all turned around now. Let me find the vendor."

God, he wanted to enjoy her laughter, not half pay attention while he determined if he was going to have to make a run for it and leave her wondering what the hell was going on.

He let out a breath of relief when they turned away. Still, he had to get out of there before they found him.

"It's this way." Nadine's search for scones fortunately pulled them in the opposite direction of his pursuers. "You haven't lived until you've enjoyed one with fresh preserves."

He positioned himself in line at the scone booth, careful to watch but doing his best to look casual. Nadine stole a glance, smiling a shy smile, touchingly sweet.

"It really is good to see you in person. I love our online communication, but it's not the same as face-to-face."

It was nice to know the time he'd poured into the emails he'd sent had been worth it. The guys had teased him that he carried his laptop around so much that he'd become an author.

"It is special," he murmured. Should've been much more special.

Damn it. He needed a neon sign for himself: *Grade-A bastard.*

They picked up scones, and he bit into one immediately. "Oh, that's good." And not because he was half starved.

Her eyes twinkled. "I told you so."

He glanced around. He didn't see either man, but he couldn't continue to waste time here.

"So, uh, my car . . ." he started, trying to come up with an excuse for why he needed to leave again.

She surprised him by stepping closer. "Would you like to come to my house for dinner? I have all this fresh food. It's been a long time since I've cooked for more than myself, so that'll be nice."

Under any other circumstances he would love to go. But now? "Um, I don't . . ."

She touched his arm. "You can relax for a few minutes. I hate to see you look so tired. You'll be safe, I promise."

She meant it as a joke, but he realized she was right. He knew where she lived—it was literally in the middle of nowhere. If he could get them out of the market without being followed, they would be safe at her place. He could rest.

One of the men rounded the last of the booths in front

of them, looking back and forth. He and his partner had split up again. The other guy might be behind them right now.

Leaving with Nadine before he was spotted would be the smartest, most tactical thing to do.

But it made him feel like a jackass.

"You know what? I would love to go to your house for dinner."

Her face lit up, filling him with more self-loathing. "Really?"

From the corner of his eye, he saw the thug's bald head bobbing up and down among so many others. He was getting closer. "Absolutely. You'll have to give me a ride though, since my car's still out of commission."

"Of course. I'll drive you back into town after dinner."

"That sounds great. Let's go." He took her by the arm, walking at a quicker pace than normal but not so much that it would draw attention. Hopefully, Nadine would attribute it to excitement over a meal with her.

Which, damn it, he *was* excited about, but he needed to not get them both killed first.

He looked to his left just in time to find the bald man smirking at him. So much for not being spotted.

He immediately shifted so that Nadine was on the side away from the goon. If he went for his gun, Wyatt didn't want her in the line of fire. And he didn't want her face exposed to them.

He saw a bench and sat her on it. "I've got to use the restroom before we leave. You sit here and do nothing but smell your pretty flowers." He pushed the roses gently toward her face, hoping she'd keep them there. "I'll be right back."

He was gone before she could reply, weaving his way through the crowds back toward the men's room. He didn't try to hide himself at all. He wanted the bad guys to see him and come after *him*, not Nadine. When he caught both of them closing in on him from either side, he smiled and didn't slow down. They'd be expecting him to try to get away.

He ran the final dozen yards to the men's room, knowing the guys would rush after him. Thankfully, the restroom was empty. Wyatt hurried into the last stall.

Within moments, the bathroom door opened with a bang as it rebounded off the tiled wall. "We know you're in here. Let's get this over with, huh? Stop wasting time. All we want is the drive. You can go free."

He didn't believe that for a second.

Wyatt slowly unlocked the door before climbing silently onto the toilet. The man opened the first stall. The second. Wyatt was in the third.

And he was ready.

The door swung open, and Wyatt grabbed hold of the metal partitions on either side of him, bracing himself, swinging his legs out and driving his boots into the man's chest.

The impact sent the guy falling back against the sinks, dazed. Wyatt jumped to the floor, ignoring his aching body's cry of protest, and turned to face Bald Guy. Wyatt ducked to miss a swing that would have probably knocked him unconscious, and returned with an uppercut and a hook that sent the guy down. He grabbed Bald Guy by the collar and slammed his fist into the man's face again.

He needed these guys knocked out long enough to get out of here with Nadine.

The first guy was trying to get up, but Wyatt rammed the side of the man's head into the ceramic sink, then watched him fall. He took a few moments to drag the men into the stalls. So long as nobody tried to open the door, it would be fine for a while.

He checked the drive in his inner jacket pocket to make sure it was okay. It looked a little dinged, but the LED light was blinking, so it must still be intact. He switched the power off, unsure how long its battery would last or what would happen to the info on it if the battery died. He needed to get the damned thing to Kendrick.

But he needed to get out of here first.

He washed his hands to get rid of the fresh blood before he hurried back out to where Nadine waited. She still had her flowers near her face like he'd asked.

The worry that clouded her eyes slid away when she saw him. "Ready?"

He grabbed the grocery bags and held a hand out in front of him. "Can't wait."

Her dazzling smile was like a punch to the gut.

Grade-A bastard.

Chapter 5

Nadine gripped the steering wheel in her hands until her knuckles turned white. She glanced at Wyatt, careful to not make it look like she was doing so.

What the hell was she doing?

She hadn't been able to resist inviting Wyatt for dinner. He'd seemed tired and a little overwrought—eyes constantly darting around the market like he expected some ninja to jump out from behind one of the plant stands and attack.

He'd mentioned in some of his emails over the years that crowds weren't his favorite. She could certainly identify with that. So she'd wanted to get him out of a situation where he was uncomfortable. A meal seemed like the most natural way.

Who was she kidding? From the second she'd heard his voice, she hadn't wanted him to leave. So he may need a home-cooked meal, but that was merely an excuse to spend more time with him face-to-face.

Chloe had told her to get back in the game. Well, she was certainly doing that.

Wyatt had told her he hadn't talked to Chloe, but Nadine had double-checked while he'd been in the restroom.

Did you take matters into your own hands and contact Wyatt?

Nadine hadn't seen how that would be possible since she'd been on the phone with Chloe right up until she'd left for the market.

Chloe quickly replied.

No . . . Do you want me to? <heart eyes emoji><heart eyes emoji> <heart eyes emoji> I'm sure Shane would have no problem setting up something.

Nadine had rolled her eyes and responded before Chloe could jump the gun. *No. I'll handle it.*

Are you sure?

Are you sure? That was the real question, wasn't it?

She had no idea. But it seemed like fate was stepping in, and for once, Nadine was going to go with it.

Yeah, I'm sure. About to drive home. Love you. TTYL.

But now she wasn't so sure. It was subtle, but much like he had at the market, he kept looking around—in the side mirror, over his shoulder, past her to the cars traveling next to them.

"Um, everything okay?"

"Yeah, fine." He shrugged one broad shoulder, and his blue button-down shirt pulled against the muscles there. She had to force her eyes away from his chest and back to the road.

And somehow remember how to breathe. And not crash.

And not turn into some stuttering idiot around him. Just because he was so much bigger and stronger and way better looking than she had remembered didn't mean she needed to start acting like her IQ had dropped thirty points.

This was the same Wyatt she'd been talking to online every week for more than two years. She could talk to him face-to-face.

"I guess being aware of your surroundings is a holdover from your time in Special Forces, huh?" She kept her eyes glued to the road.

"What makes you say that?"

He sounded tense. Maybe this was the wrong thing to bring up. "You keep looking around. That's why I asked if everything was okay."

He let out a breath and eased his head back against the seat. He shifted the jacket folded over his lap. "I'm sorry. You're right. Sometimes it's tough to shut down that part of my brain . . . old habits, I guess."

"I mean, it makes sense. Plus your job with Linear now. You're used to keeping an eye on your surroundings. Most jobs don't require that."

"You mean you don't look over your shoulder all the time as a virtual assistant? Setting up travel arrangements sounds pretty dangerous." A half smile curved those full, firm lips.

Her eyes shot back to the road in front of her. No looking at his lips. No *thinking* about his lips. "Only when I don't manage to score priority boarding."

He laughed and she relaxed. It felt good, making him laugh. They fell into an easy conversation the way they had with their online chats. As they got farther out of town, he seemed to relax too. He still glanced in the mirrors every once in a while, but not as often. Probably because he'd realized there was no way trouble could find them out on this empty highway without them realizing it.

She wanted to give him a night where he could relax. She didn't know if he understood how much his friendship had meant to her since the incident. Besides Chloe, he was the only person she'd had any sort of regular contact with on a personal basis.

She could admit she wasn't doing great with the whole face-to-face interpersonal interaction part of her life . . . but she couldn't imagine where she'd be emotionally if it weren't for him.

So she'd give him a nice night.

She wasn't going to worry about what his words or actions meant—whether he was flirting or not. He had seemed to stay closer to her than necessary at the market—touching her, guiding her, poking her gently.

Maybe that was flirting, or maybe it was the way he was with women. Maybe it didn't mean anything.

She wasn't going to worry about how bad she was at all this. She would focus on the good.

Like their conversation. That had always been good no matter how they talked: chat room, email, phone. They had a good rhythm. And she was glad to see that was true face-to-face also.

Before she knew it, she was pulling up in front of the little brick bungalow she called home. Good thing she had cleaned over the weekend.

"Here we are. It's not much, but it's mine."

He studied the house, then glanced at her. "I like it. Perfect size for one person too."

Unfolding his long body, he climbed out of the car. "Let me get that." He took the two bags full of produce while she carried the flowers.

She stopped to unlock the door, aware of him behind her. It was rare to meet a man who made her feel small. At five ten, she was taller than every other woman she knew and had worn flats on dates her whole life. Wyatt still towered over her.

"Do you like being so far outside of town?" he asked. "I know I would love the quiet out here."

"That's what I was looking for. Peace and quiet."

"Do you ever miss being around people?"

She gave him a wry chuckle. "You sound like Chloe.

Except she doesn't bother asking that question. She assumes I must be miserable without people, but I'm not."

Opening the front door, she knew she had to admit the full truth. He would understand. He always did. "I do miss being around people sometimes. I used to love the energy on set back at *Day's End*. There was so much creativity. Collaboration. People bouncing their ideas off each other."

"Until Oakley ruined it for you."

Her stomach clenched at Travis's name. Of course, Wyatt knew it. He'd seen her in the hospital, and they'd talked about it a little bit since.

She forced herself to keep walking and lead Wyatt to the kitchen, busying herself finding vases for the flowers while he put the grocery bags on the counter. She hoped he wouldn't notice her silence.

But he did. "Still don't like hearing his name?"

She sighed. "I don't think I'm ever going to like hearing his name. I don't even like thinking about him. I spend a lot of time *not* thinking about him."

She never wanted to think about him again.

"Can I tell you something I learned in the Special Forces?"

"Sure." They certainly knew each other well enough for him to give her advice. And frankly, anything delivered in his deep voice would be worth hearing.

He began unloading the market purchases from the bag. "Never turn your back on your enemy if you have any choice. In this case, that's the memories of Oakley. Turning your back won't make them go away. All it does is make you more vulnerable. You've got to process it so you can figure out how to move on."

Move on.

It was all she really wanted. But Wyatt didn't know the whole truth, nobody did. He didn't know that Nadine sometimes still woke up screaming because of what Travis had done.

How he'd left her to die.

Wyatt didn't know how the sensation of choking on her own blood tore her from her sleep, how she'd gasp for air and claw at her throat like she was right back in that burning cabin. How the smell of her own flesh burning sometimes had her running for the toilet to retch.

She glanced down at her legs, glad she'd gone with jeans. He knew about her scars, but seeing her deformed flesh would probably have taken him aback.

"Moving on doesn't mean I forget," she said softly. "I don't get to forget everything so easily. My reminders are inescapable. I don't know if I'll ever be completely over it."

He laid the rest of the fresh produce on the counter. "There are some things a person never fully gets over, and that's okay."

"Tell that to Chloe." She grabbed the cherries and lettuce and placed them inside the fridge. "She's moved on, even though what happened to her was worse. She's healed. Has no problem with it anymore."

"People heal at different rates. It's not a race." His voice was calm, steady.

She closed the fridge, staring at the door because it was easier than looking him in the eye. "I don't see how I'm supposed to heal when I'm still afraid of getting hurt."

"Physically or emotionally?"

She still didn't look at him. "Both."

"That's okay. Fear has kept me and my friends alive more than once."

She doubted it was the same thing at all. But she didn't want to concentrate on that tonight. She wanted to have a meal with a gorgeous man and help him relax a little. Help them *both* relax a little.

She blew out a breath and changed the subject. "So, how does pasta primavera sound? All this produce I got at the market will be put to good use."

He grinned, and she was glad he wasn't going to push the issue. "What do you need from me?"

"That's the perfect response." They shared a laugh while she gathered the ingredients. He washed up, then started to chop the zucchini, onions, and tomatoes.

They worked side by side with her washing veggies for him to chop. "You're pretty good with a knife," she noted.

"Thank you. Occupational hazard, I guess."

Her eyes got big. She'd never thought of it that way. "Really?"

He nudged her. "That was a joke. This is a far cry from using a knife on an adversary, trust me. I had to teach myself some basic cooking skills or else there'd be nothing in my trash can but crumpled-up fast food bags."

"I've always loved to cook . . . and eat," she added with a laugh at herself. Nobody would ever have called her petite. She was a big girl and had been for as long as she could remember. Always taller, always wider.

Solid was how she'd always been described, which somehow was more insulting than it was meant to be.

"Nothing wrong with that." He winked and tapped her on the nose before he went back to chopping.

She kept looking at him while he chopped. Was he flirting or merely being friendly?

Friendly, right? Someone like Wyatt could have any woman he wanted. She doubted that would be the scarred, antisocial, *big* girl.

She pushed the thoughts aside. He was here and they were having a nice time. That was all that mattered. She wouldn't let herself lose the present moment in favor of questioning every little thing.

The conversation was light throughout their colorful dinner. He gushed about the food so much she actually blushed. He still seemed exhausted—a bone-deep weariness, not a normal so-tired-of-meetings fatigue. She wanted to ask him about it but didn't push.

Instead, she concentrated on stuff she really shouldn't. Stuff she'd been able to ignore when they were pen pals. Like how ruggedly handsome he was in a way that made her insides melt. How his brown eyes, a deep, luscious caramel, drew her in. And always how big and strong he was, with thick, corded muscle pushing against the seams of his shirt. How it made her feel almost delicate, something she'd never thought she'd feel.

But it was more than that. She *liked* him. She liked talking to him, listening to him, and joking with him. Even without his good looks, she'd still be happy to share a meal with him.

And her goal of keeping things light for both of them was working. He seemed relaxed as they ate, telling her stories about his family. He'd mentioned them before in their talks, so she knew he had a younger brother and sister and how close they were in age. A tale of them at the beach for a family vacation—Wyatt convincing his five-year-old brother he had to pee on the seashells he'd collected to get rid of the shark poop—had her in stitches.

"How about you?" he asked as he got them both a second helping of pasta. "I guess there weren't a lot of childhood vacations in foster care."

She shook her head. "Not many. But Chloe and I have more than made up for it as adults. We've traveled all over the place."

Although not for the past two years. Yet another thing she'd let Travis steal from her.

"Chloe's like a sister to you."

Nadine forked a piece of zucchini. "She is my sister in every way that matters." She shrugged. "I guess that sounds weird to someone who has actual siblings."

"Not at all. The Linear Tactical guys are every bit as much my brothers as Mickey is. I'd do anything for them, and I know the feeling's mutual."

"Exactly."

"Speaking of Chloe, why were you asking if I'd been talking to her earlier?"

Dang it. She took another bite, wishing she could avoid the question. "You won't laugh at me?"

"Oh, now I'm intrigued." He rested his chin on his hands and waggled his eyebrows, making her feel a little less stupid. She smiled.

"Chloe and I were talking on the phone earlier . . . about you." She pushed pasta around on her plate.

"Me? Wow. Flattering things, I hope?"

Canoodling. Nadine fought not to flush, but looking at the table made it worse. "She, uh . . . was encouraging me to be more open with you. Make some plans to meet face-to-face rather than just talk online."

"Looks like we have that out of the way already."

"Yep. And she was doing her damnedest to convince me it would be a good idea to ask if you'd like to meet up for coffee sometime or . . . a date." She was unable to keep eye contact with him. "She knows how much talking with you has meant to me. How much I look forward to hearing from you."

His hand covered hers. "Same here."

She looked up at him again, and his sexy half-smile curled her toes. "Then, right after she and I had that conversation, you showed up out of nowhere." She cleared her throat. Couldn't believe what she was about to say. "I'd say that's a sign, wouldn't you?"

"A sign?"

It was time to take a chance. "That the universe wanted to help you and me out. Today, I told my best friend I'd be willing to go out with you if . . . things progressed in that direction. I was going to try to figure out a way to suggest we meet in person." Her words came out in a rush, but she couldn't help it. *Be brave. Be brave. Keep going.* "And then you showed up at the market. If that's not a sign, I don't know what is."

His hand slid off hers and he sat up a little straighter. "A sign . . . Right."

She nodded. "What happened today is kind of crazy. The market is the only place I go to regularly, and only on Mondays. If you'd been there any other day or gone anywhere else in town—hell, anywhere else in Idaho at *all*—you wouldn't have seen me." She shrugged. "It seemed like the universe was trying to help us out. Push us in a direction."

With every second he didn't say anything, just sat chewing his food, she felt more like an idiot.

Finally he nodded but then launched into another story, this time about his sister chasing him around the house with a baseball bat because he'd drawn a moustache on one of her American Girl dolls.

Nadine laughed at the funny parts and winced as he explained all the extra chores he'd had to do to replace the doll—much more expensive than the ten-year-old had expected. But she was aware of the differences from the stories now than the ones he told before.

The light was gone from behind his eyes. His smile lacked something.

She shouldn't have said what she had. Things were awkward between them now. Obviously, he hadn't attached any universal significance to them meeting at the market.

It was stupid that she had. The universe wasn't pushing them together. And there was definitely no talk about going out on a date.

They finished their meal, the conversation between them flowing, but lacking the magic from earlier. She stood and grabbed their plates to walk them to the sink. "I've got some ice cream if you're a fan."

He winced as he stood and grabbed their glasses.

God, was it that bad that he was wincing at the thought of having to spend more time with her?

"Or not," she managed to get out brightly. "You probably need to get back to town. It's no problem."

Well, at least now she had her answer about whether Wyatt was interested in a more intimate relationship.

He wasn't.

Chapter 6

Wyatt pushed down the aches coursing through his body as he stood, silently cursing the shadow that fell over Nadine's face. As if he needed to feel any more like a jackass.

Evidently, it wasn't enough to know he was using this sweet, charming, funny, beautiful woman for his own gain.

Now he had to know she'd taken their little run-in as a sign from the universe. Like she was on the right track and her life was finally beginning to turn around.

Shit.

She was finally ready to stick her chin out and see what life had to offer. He'd been waiting as patiently as he could—and that had been so fucking hard, given how he felt about her—for her to reach this point. To make a real, actual move toward wanting more out of their old-fashioned courtship.

But her thinking him showing up today as a sign from the universe? He wished he could reach his own ass to kick it.

Worse was the way she carefully avoided looking at him. She looked everywhere but at him—the dishes in the sink, her shoes, the counter. They'd had such a wonderful meal, talking and laughing in ways that had helped him forget everything for a few minutes. To give his brain and body a much-needed respite.

Even without what had happened to Frank and the constantly frantic pace since, Wyatt had never been a charming, relaxed person. He'd never been one to share about himself.

But he could relax around Nadine. Had relaxed—almost ridiculously so, given the circumstances—right up to the point where she'd started talking about how the two of them meeting today was *fate*.

There was so much of this situation, so much of their relationship in general, she didn't know. Way too much.

She deserved better than this.

She deserved to be set up on the counter and kissed until she couldn't remember her own name. His hands almost itched with the need to do that. To kiss and touch her and forget everything else. To lose himself in this woman who'd captivated him without trying.

But it wasn't an option, not right now. Not with so many lies between them. Especially not until he figured out how to handle the situation with the computer drive and the people willing to kill for it.

But there was no way he could live with the hurt in her eyes right now, knowing he'd put it there. Knowing she was thinking he didn't want anything to do with her.

"Hey. I'm sorry." He pulled her away from the dishes and cupped her cheeks with his hands, forcing those hazel eyes to look up at him. "I messed up earlier. I hurt you and I'm sorry. There's nothing more I want than to agree the universe brought us together today, but I'm not sure I believe in that sort of thing."

And all the rest. All the secrets he was keeping.

She would've turned away, but he wouldn't let her. "But one thing I definitely know?" he continued. "Being with you today has been amazing. You're smart and funny, and I won't deny that the way you cook makes me want to hire you as my personal chef. This has been a great day. The greatest day."

"Really?"

God, he hated the doubt in her voice. He trailed his thumbs down her cheek. "Without a doubt."

He'd had to tell her so many lies today, but every single word of this was the truth.

He pulled her in for a hug, relieved when she didn't pull away. "Getting to know you over the past two years has been the highlight of my life."

"Really?" she asked again, her question muffled by his shoulder.

"Truest words I've ever spoken."

She snuggled closer, and he had to swallow a groan as his arms automatically tightened around her. Holding her like this was beyond good. She fit perfectly against him, like they were made for each other. He was a big guy, nearly six foot four, and he dwarfed most women. Not Nadine. She was substantial, Amazon warrior woman sized, and he fucking loved it. He had no time for skinny waifs.

But he'd made a tactical error holding her this close, her ample curves nestling against him. She was soft, warm, *lush*. Her body held endless wonders he'd love nothing more than to indulge in.

But not right now. He couldn't let this go in that direction, no matter how much he wanted to. Things were bad enough as it was.

But he kept her against him a few moments longer. How many nights had he dreamed about doing this very thing? Finally, he pulled back, loving the way her eyes shone up at him. She was a little breathless.

God, if she only knew what she did to him.

"So." She stepped back and turned to the dishes in the sink, washing them. He picked up a towel to dry what she handed him.

"So." He needed to change the subject. No more talk of fate or the universe smiling on them. He couldn't bear it. Not with all the lies between them. "I like your house. Like all the space around it. How far is your nearest neighbor?"

"Over three miles away. It took a little getting used to at first, but it wasn't long before this place really started to help me."

"The house itself, or the land?"

Her little bungalow wasn't very large, but it was homey. Probably two bedrooms, given the size. He'd only seen the living room and the kitchen with its dining nook, but it was clear she'd taken a plain property and made it her own.

Flowers from the market, but also colorful throws and pillows on her leather couch to add pops of color against the white walls. An oversized plush chair by one of the huge back windows, a stack of books beside it. Obviously, a favorite reading spot.

"Both, probably." She handed him another plate to dry. "I like being here. I like that no one knows where this is or would take the time to come out to the least populous town in Idaho, even if they did. But it's this area—the land itself— that has really helped me the most."

"That I definitely can understand. The Wyoming wilderness has calmed the beast inside me on many a night. Chased the nightmares away."

She looked over with agreement clear in her eyes. "I've been soaking it up as much as possible. Getting outside more and more. Mostly hiking, and believe it or not, some kayaking and rappelling."

Her soft voice was making it harder not to push her up

against the counter and kiss them both senseless. "You liked rappelling, huh?"

"I never thought I would be the type of person to go over a cliff on purpose. But . . . yeah, I like it. Like facing my fears and not letting them stop me."

He understood that right down to his bones. "You like being in control."

"There's been a lot in my life I haven't been in control of, so yeah, rappelling makes me feel . . . strong." She shrugged. "Yeah. Maybe I'm trying to get past some old fears."

She was strong. So much stronger than she realized. Unfortunately, that wasn't something someone else could tell her with any real effect. She had to figure it out for herself.

She went back to washing a glass. "It helps that after the initial learning, they aren't group activities," she added. "I like my solitude."

"You should come out to Oak Creek sometime. The beauty of our outdoors rivals yours. Plus, being outside is part of our business."

"Really?"

"Sure. A big part of what we do at Linear Tactical is wilderness survival training."

Her eyes lit up. "You never told me that. What do you teach?"

He turned and leaned against the counter so he could see her while he dried. "We teach a modified version of the SERE training we learned in the military."

"Sear?"

"S-E-R-E. Survival. Evasion. Resistance. Escape. It's a type of training a lot of military members go through. The air force established it at the end of World War II, but the other branches have picked it up. Survival training for warfare situations."

"You guys teach that to people?"

"Basically. We focus on the survival aspect since most people aren't trying to evade captors or live through prisoner-of-war situations. Stuff like building a shelter, how to start and maintain a fire, how to set up traps and snares."

"Really?" Her eyes lit up as she finished the last of the dishes and went to get the ice cream out of the freezer. He nodded enthusiastically when she showed him the container.

"We get groups who come, but also individuals. Some people want to learn in case of emergencies. Others want to build on skills they already have."

She scooped out ice cream and handed him a bowl. "How long are the courses?"

He loved that she was so interested in this. "Everything from a single day to two full weeks. We can teach a few basics over a weekend, like improvising equipment and making it out of what can be found nearby. How to navigate. How to tell dangerous vegetation from the rest."

"Wow, that's exciting stuff."

"And necessary. Between all the hikers and climbers around there, they need to know how to survive if things go south. We also teach the basics of evasion—how to gain a tactical advantage over an opponent. You'd be surprised how many people are interested in that."

"Actually, I'm not surprised at all. I would love to learn about that."

He grinned. "You'll have to come to Oak Creek some time, then. Take a course."

She leaned against the counter, tipping her spoon upside down and licking it.

Jesus.

Watching that sweet pink tongue lick down the length of the metal had him all but groaning. To make it worse, it was a totally innocent gesture on her part. She was just deep in thought about SERE training and enjoying her ice cream.

He, on the other hand, would love to use their tongues to trail up and down the lengths of each other's body.

"Do you ever teach the classes?"

He tore his gaze away from her mouth. "Sometimes. I'll make sure I'm the one who teaches you. How's that sound?"

Her cheeks flushed. *So pretty.* How far down did that flush go? "That sounds good."

He pointed his spoon at her. "I'll hold you to it. And don't think I'll forget."

"I wouldn't let you."

They finished their dessert with more talk about wilderness survival training. They stayed in the kitchen, their conversation as informal as the room itself. He'd love to stay here and talk until morning.

He'd love to take her back to the bedroom too. He'd love to explore those curves that had been driving him crazy all night. He'd be equally happy with the talking.

But right now, he needed to cut both off. It was time to head back to town and contact Kendrick Foster, Linear Tactical's computer guru, with the burner phone she'd let him plug in to charge when they'd first arrived home. He'd had his reprieve. Gotten more than he needed or deserved from her company.

Which had him sighing as they finished washing and drying the ice cream bowls. "I guess—"

"You need to go," she finished for him. "I understand. You've escaped what's hounding you long enough, and now you have to go back and face it."

He did a double take. "What?" That was way too close to the truth.

"It just seemed like you've relaxed for your given amount of time, and now you have to go back and fight the bad guys." She glanced down, embarrassed. "Don't listen to me. I have an overactive imagination."

The woman was damn near perfect. Insightful, but sweet and generous to a fault. No wonder it had been easy for Oakley to take advantage of her.

So easy for *him* to take advantage of her, and it didn't matter if it was for better reasons.

He neither confirmed nor denied her observation, although he wanted nothing more than to tell her that her instincts were spot on. "I've loved hanging out with you tonight, Nadine. Everything about it was amazing, especially the company."

She gave him a little nod, and they walked out to her car, both admiring the stars in the clear, crisp night.

His hands twitched from the impulse to reach for her, but he tamped it down. Another time.

The ride back to town was pleasant enough, but tension filled him with each mile closer to civilization. The killers knew he'd have to steal a car, so they'd be checking for those reports. When they didn't find any, they'd start checking places he'd try to hitch a ride.

"Do you want me to take you to the mechanic's? They can't possibly be open at this hour."

Right. The reason he supposedly had to hang around town earlier. "I'm staying at a hotel for the night."

He directed her to a hotel on the town's outskirts, blocks from the market. "This is the one."

Once she was gone, he'd sneak back out and figure out a plan.

She pulled up at the curb and put the car in park before turning to him. "Thank you for today."

"You're the one who deserves the thanks. For dinner, for the excellent company, for carting me back and forth. You made this a good day." Given his mind a chance to rest, his body a chance to relax, although the pain still made him stiff.

She'd probably saved his life and would never know it.

He might never be able to talk to her about any of this, and he regretted there would always be lies between them. But he definitely planned to see her again as soon as he could. Being around her had made that a priority.

But it might be weeks from now, and he fucking hated that. And he wouldn't be able to explain why.

He reached over and kissed her cheek, breathing in her sweet scent. "Thank you. I mean it. I'll message you soon."

"Okay. Be safe." She stayed as he got out of the car and walked toward the sliding doors leading into the hotel. It would be easier if she'd drive away so he could give up the ruse, but he didn't have that luck. He'd have to go inside and head toward the front desk like he was a guest here.

The doors opened. He glanced over his shoulder and found her waiting. He gave her a little wave, then walked inside.

He saw them as soon as he entered the lobby. He didn't stop his stride or give any outward indication that he'd noticed the two men. One was in a chair reading a magazine while the other was leaning against a long console table talking on the phone.

Pretending to talk on the phone.

Neither of them made overt moves that gave them away, perhaps a split second too long of interest. If it weren't for Wyatt's training—years of walking into missions where innocents and enemies had to be identified at a moment's notice —he might not have noticed them either.

These weren't the same men who'd been hunting him in the market today, but they definitely had the same purpose— to retrieve the computer drive.

This town wasn't very big. There were probably similar teams placed at any other hotels, waiting to see if Wyatt appeared.

It wouldn't be long until those teams were here.

A couple walked by. Wyatt kept his eye on the two men as he stepped back, forcing the couple to cross in front of him. He hadn't been joking when he'd told Nadine not to turn her back on the enemy.

The lady muttered an apology as she brushed by him, but they kept walking out the door. The two men hadn't moved, but the clock was already ticking. He needed to get out of here.

Had Nadine already left? He didn't want to do anything that would draw their attention to her. He would head upstairs, then sneak back down, going out a back door, not caring if it would set off alarms.

He walked briskly to the elevator and jabbed his thumb on the button, then glanced at the two men. They weren't following yet. That was good. The doors opened right away, and he swayed the slightest bit as he entered, his vision going a little blurry.

He blinked twice. What just happened?

The doors closed behind him without anyone approaching, which was suspicious in itself. He'd expected to be participating in close-quarters combat when the two guys got on the elevator with him.

He reached to press the third-floor button, but the numbers blurred in front of his eyes.

Shit. He'd been drugged.

The woman who'd brushed against him as she'd passed him in the lobby. She'd gotten something into his system through his skin.

He braced himself against the wall as the elevator moved, stopped, and the doors slid open. Everything was getting worse. Blurry, uneven.

Staggering down the hall, he kept the red exit sign in his crosshairs. Nothing mattered as much as getting out of this building. He was going to be unconscious soon, and his chance of survival would drop to zero once that happened.

He pushed himself along the wall, one lurching step at a time, before he finally made it into the stairwell. He somehow made it back down the first turn of stairs, his grip on the handrail the only thing keeping him on his feet.

"There you are. My boss wants to have a talk with you."

There was no way Wyatt was going to make it out of this.

Chapter 7

Nadine should leave.

She should put the car into drive and pull away. Why was she sitting here staring at the hotel that Wyatt had walked into a few minutes ago?

Because she was a coward.

No matter how she flinched at the thought, it was true. The whole night, she'd wanted to kiss him, had kept inching toward him, but had pulled back every time the possibility got too close.

When would she see him again? Except for that one part of the conversation where things had gone awkwardly silent, they hadn't really talked about them taking things forward. Did he have a clue she wanted to see him as more than a dinner buddy?

He didn't believe the universe had brought them together. Fine, maybe she didn't either. But the fact that he had shown up at that market right after she and Chloe talked about him? That had to be more than sheer coincidence.

Chloe heard voices in her head all the time. After two decades of being around Chloe as that happened, Nadine had long since given up on thinking it was weird. It was the way Chloe's brain worked.

Some things couldn't be easily explained.

So Nadine wasn't going to find it too odd that the universe had dropped the sexy, intelligent, honest man she hadn't been able to get out of her mind for years into her lap right as she was ready to move forward with her life.

She should've kissed him. There in the kitchen when she could've sworn he'd wanted it too. She should've grabbed him by those broad shoulders and pulled him to her. But she'd chickened out and missed her chance.

But damn, it wasn't too late to be brave for once, to be bold. To park this damn car, follow him into that hotel, and kiss him.

She wasn't trying to rush things. Just one single kiss. A real kiss. That's all she wanted right now.

Sure, she wanted more than that. Wanted all the . . . *canoodling*. But for now, a kiss would be enough.

She parked and rushed into the lobby, pulling out her phone. He had probably barely gotten to his room. He could easily come back down, couldn't he? She texted him.

I'm in the lobby. Can I see you for a minute?

Ugh. That wasn't really very casual, was it? But she definitely wasn't going to ask him if she could come up to his room—that would give off a very different, *noncasual* vibe.

She kept staring at her phone, willing him to text her back. But there was nothing. He'd been out of the car less than three minutes. Maybe he was talking to someone and couldn't respond.

What should she do? Wimp out and go home, or stick around until he showed up?

Brave. Bold. Not a coward.

She'd wait here, at least for a few minutes—sit in the lobby, be casual. When she turned, two men had moved to stand by the door. It didn't take an expert in body language to know they were waiting for somebody, watching for them. They were communicating silently via curt hand gestures to another man sitting in the lobby who was pretending to read a magazine.

Maybe it was all the discussion about the SERE training, or talking about Travis, or her overworked imagination, but something wasn't right here.

They weren't paying any attention to her, thankfully, but they were watching and waiting for someone. The one with the magazine kept turning to look over his shoulder, down the hall.

She shot another text to Wyatt. *Are you okay? Please let me know.*

Still nothing. She wasn't leaving here without knowing Wyatt was all right. She went to the front desk, where a young woman clearly thought there was something weird about the men too. She kept looking up at them from under her lashes, pretending to be busy with work.

"Hi." Nadine gave her a tight smile. "I wonder if you could help me. A friend of mine just checked in, and I need to see him. Could you call his room?"

"Sure." The girl glanced at the men again before she turned to her computer. "What's his name?"

"Wyatt Highfield."

Out of the corner of her eye, she saw the two men stand at attention. They might as well have been dogs whose ears had perked up. They recognized the name. Oh God.

"I don't have that name in our system," the girl murmured. "You said Highfield?"

Nadine nodded. She felt eyes boring into her back. What was going on here? She'd watched him walk into the hotel. He hadn't come back out.

What if he'd had to make a quick escape? What if those

men were here for him and he saw them before they noticed him?

Maybe she was crazy and was letting her imagination run away with her. It was more likely he'd used another name. He was in the security business, after all. There could've been a reason for him to travel incognito.

Which meant she might have blown his cover.

She forced a smile. "Oh well. Must be a lag in the system. I'll keep waiting and texting. He'll be down here any minute." She raised her voice enough to be sure the men heard her.

Before turning away, she asked, "Where's your restroom?" The clerk pointed to the very obvious doors on the other side of the lobby. She'd already noticed the doors, but if the men were listening, she wanted them to think she was heading there.

And hope they didn't follow.

They didn't. The two were still muttering to each other. She ducked past the restrooms and down the hall, jogging to the back stairwell once she was out of sight. She went inside and paused to catch her breath. Everything was happening so fast, and she didn't have the first idea what any of it meant.

She needed to get out of here while they weren't watching her and find a way to get in touch with Wyatt.

Muffled sounds above her made her head snap up, her eyes searching the stairs above her. Sound carried easily in these places, so she didn't know how far above the people were.

But she sure as hell knew it was a fight.

She wanted no part of it and was about to duck back out when she froze. That was Wyatt's voice.

Or . . . some bizarro version of it. He sounded like he

was drunk. And like he was getting the crap beaten out of him.

She could go back to the lobby and have the clerk call the police for help, or maybe grab a security guard. But there hadn't been any out there, had there? How long would it take for help to arrive, especially with more suspicious looking guys in the lobby?

She couldn't do nothing. She needed to help.

Another sickening sound of flesh hitting flesh. Wyatt groaned.

"You're going to tell us what we want to know," the man sneered. "I was only supposed to escort you out, but I wanted to get a few good blows in myself for making us chase you for three fucking days. Once we get you back to the boss, I'll have to wait my turn to kick the shit out of you some more."

Another punch. Wyatt's mumbled response was indecipherable. God, he must be badly hurt if he couldn't form a sentence.

Damn it, she had to help right now. There was pepper spray in her purse, which was better than nothing. She grabbed for it and ran up the stairs.

She found them two floors up. A tall, overweight man stepped back with a snicker as Wyatt swung for him and completely missed. The swing knocked him off-balance and Wyatt fell against the wall.

There was definitely something wrong with him. She'd never seen him fight, but he was a trained Special Forces soldier—there was no way he was this bad.

And the other guy was taking advantage of it. He punched Wyatt square in the gut, making him double over.

And when he did, when his line of vision was closer to the floor, Wyatt caught sight of Nadine creeping up the stairs.

"No," he grunted through clenched teeth. "Run."

No way that was happening.

The attacker spun around, but she had her pepper spray raised. He threw his hands up to protect himself, but it was too late. She damn near emptied the whole can in his face.

When the guy staggered back, she took a swing at him—straight into the nose with her palm like she'd been taught in the self-defense classes Chloe had talked her into taking. She shuddered at the feel of his nose breaking under her hand and blood pouring out everywhere.

That part hadn't been covered in class.

He howled as he fell to the ground while Wyatt remained slumped against the stairs. She needed to get them out of there before broken-nose guy's buddies showed up from the lobby.

"Come on." She took him under the arms and hauled him up until he was on his feet. Finally, something good came out of her size and strength. A petite little thing couldn't have managed that.

"You've got to get away." He coughed a few times from the pepper spray, groaning when he did. He sounded disoriented. Nothing like the man who'd left her car less than ten minutes ago.

"Not without you." She had no idea what was happening, or why there were people after him. All she knew was that he was in trouble and there was no abandoning him now. She blinked her eyes against the sting. "Come on. Lean on me. We'll get you down the stairs."

But his feet didn't seem to want to obey. She practically dragged him down one lurching step at a time with her shoulder tucked into his armpit.

"Gotta . . . get away . . . safe . . . drive . . ." His words became less recognizable with each step.

There was no way in hell he was going to be able to drive in this condition.

"I'm going to get us both away if you would just walk, damn it. Help me, please." He seemed to try to move his feet, to bear his weight. It was better than nothing, anyway.

They reached the big, metal door at the bottom of the stairwell, which led outside. She pushed her way through and pulled Wyatt along with her. They were behind the hotel now, next to a row of dumpsters.

"I've got to get you to a doctor. A hospital. You're hurt. Poisoned or something."

"No. No." He pulled her to a stop. "No doctor. No hospital."

"Wyatt, you need help."

He shook his head. "Drugged," he slurred. "Wear off."

"Drugged." She didn't know who those guys in the lobby were, or the one she'd sprayed, and there was no point in demanding to know now. She started dragging Wyatt toward her car again. Whoever they were, they'd be looking for him soon.

"I need . . ." His head started to droop. His legs began to buckle, dragging her down.

"No. Wyatt, come on." She propped him against the wall and slapped his cheek, wincing, knowing he'd taken punches to his face.

His eyes opened. "What? What?" He sounded angry— not that she minded. As long as he was awake.

"Stay with me." She started walking them again. She wouldn't have very long before he got pulled under. "Finish what you were trying to tell me. You said you have to get away from here, and you need something. What do you need?"

"Hide. Hide. Sleep." It sounded like every word was a struggle.

"Hide from who?"

He shook his head and they stumbled a few more steps. She kept them away from the windows in the lobby. "Didn't. Want. Tell you."

She didn't know what he was talking about. "Let's get you to the car."

"Can't. I . . ." His legs threatened to buckle again. "Leave me."

"Wyatt, come on. We need to hurry. There are men in the lobby who are going to come after you."

"Not. Safe." He stopped moving again. "You. Go."

Damn it. She needed another tactic. "Those guys in the lobby are going to get me if you don't get to my car, Wyatt. The only way for me to get out of here is for you to get to my car."

Her risk paid off. She could almost see the superhuman effort he made to focus. To command his body to do what he was telling it to do.

Because he wanted to protect *her*.

"Let's go." They were the clearest words she'd heard from him yet.

He still needed help, but at least he was making a focused effort. They shuffled across the parking lot toward her car. She practically shoved him into the back seat, bending his legs and picking up his feet to tuck them in with him.

She ran around to the driver's side and started the car. "Where, Wyatt? Should I take you somewhere? Drive you to Wyoming?"

He shook his head. "Your house."

Then his head dropped to the seat.

No activity in the lobby—she could barely make out the two big, hulking figures in there. All she wanted was to floor the gas and get the hell out of there, but she couldn't attract attention.

Which was why she slowly pulled away from the hotel, driving like there wasn't an unconscious man in the back seat who'd been drugged and beaten. Like she didn't have a problem in the world.

She had wanted to start living again, hadn't she? Well the universe had listened.

Chapter 8

Consciousness came back in waves. Sounds. Sensations.

Wyatt knew to keep his eyes closed until he got his bearings. Let them think he was still out. He stayed still while he gathered all the information he could about his surroundings.

He should hear the buzzing of insects. The scratching of rats. The stench of his body and the waste he hadn't been allowed to wash off. To have to flinch away from the extreme heat of an early morning sun, the sort of heat anyone who hadn't grown up in the desert couldn't hope to adjust to easily.

He moved his ankle slightly, expecting to find it bound with a shackle.

His body ached in the way that told him the prison guards had enjoyed beating him last night the way they had all six nights since he'd been in this hellhole. Like his body had been stomped, used for sport. Not quite torture for information, but an expression of the knowledge that they held all the power and he held none.

That he'd never be leaving this Iraqi prison alive.

He tightened his shoulders against the pain, determined to find a way out, find the strength to get through this day. He shifted to see through cracked eyes . . .

And felt a pillow under his head.

Wait, that wasn't right.

Both his hands and feet were free. The room was cool, and a blanket covered him. There was no bright light on the other side of his eyelids. All was quiet.

Not completely quiet. Someone was . . . singing.

A woman's voice, soft, low, but clear.

He shuddered as his brain separated the past from the present. He wasn't in that Iraqi prison from ten years ago; he was at Nadine's house.

He still didn't open his eyes, allowing his senses to filter the information and his mind to remember.

The hotel. The people after the drive had found him.

But . . .

If Nadine had brought him back to her house and he was still in one piece, that meant she'd found a way around the people who'd drugged and attacked him.

But how?

How the hell had she gotten him past a bunch of pros? Her pretty voice crooning a ballad from a Broadway show about one of America's founding fathers assured him she'd not only gotten past the men who'd been sent to capture, torture, and kill him, but evidently she was unscathed.

He remembered seeing her in the stairwell, wanting her to run, but not much after that.

He looked at the nightstand and saw his burner phone with the small computer drive resting next to it. He grabbed both, flipping the switch on the small drive to make sure it hadn't been damaged and felt relief when the lights on the side lit green.

He turned the switch on the drive off and texted

Kendrick. Wyatt used his military code name—and LT nickname—since Kendrick wouldn't recognize the burner phone.

Hopefully, the bad guys monitoring Linear wouldn't either.

Blaze, this is Scout. I have a gift that needs your love ASAP coming to you. More details as available.

It only took a second for the reply. *Roger. Stay safe.*

Wyatt set the phone down and the tiniest groan escaped as he tried to sit up. The singing immediately stopped as she ran into the room. "Whoa, not too fast. You're in pretty rough shape."

He grunted. His older bruises now had newer little bruises to keep them company. "Yeah."

"Which I guess is why you've been asleep for more than twenty-four hours."

"What?" Shock pushed away the cloud of foggy half-memories wrapped around him. "I've been out that whole time?"

"Yeah. It's Tuesday night, almost midnight. I got you here and into bed. I kept waiting for you to wake up, but you didn't. But you were breathing and your pulse was steady so I didn't take you to the hospital."

"Good." If she had, he'd be dead now. Maybe her too.

He realized he was almost fully undressed. "Where are my clothes?"

She looked away, then back at him, then away again. "You, um . . . couldn't seem to get comfortable, so I thought getting you out of your jeans might help."

"Not comfortable?"

She met his eyes. "You seemed to think you were in jail or something. You were . . . upset."

Shit. No wonder he'd woken up convinced he was back in that airless hellhole—evidently his mind had thought he was. His exhaustion had helped, along with the drugs and pain.

"Not prison, but I had a pretty shitty few days in an Iraqi holding cell. I think getting the crap kicked out of me reminded my subconscious of those fun times."

Her face darkened with concern. "Oh my gosh."

He kept the sheet wrapped around his hips as he swung his legs over the side of the bed and sat up. He felt dizzy, but it was manageable. "It was ten years ago. My team got me out. I was lucky."

She shook her head. "Lucky? Those nightmares didn't sound lucky."

He shrugged. "What I went through is nothing compared to what Dorian, one of my Special Forces brothers, survived. He was held for five weeks in Afghanistan. He didn't come back the same. So comparatively, I was very lucky."

She was still staring at him. "You have some . . . burn scars."

They'd burned his back twice with a fire-hot poker. He would never forget the agony of it, the smell of his flesh burning.

She'd been through so much worse. He hadn't seen her scars but had read the medical reports. A product of that bastard Oakley leaving her unconscious in a house while it burned around her.

He met her eyes. "You have burn scars too."

She shrugged. "I was unconscious for a lot of my burns."

He knew there was much more to burn pain than when it first happened, but didn't push. "Thank you for getting my clothes off. Hopefully, that made me a little more bearable."

She was standing just out of reach—more closed off and distant than she'd been during their dinner. She had to have questions.

She gestured toward his chest. "You have a lot of bruises. Some of them look older than others—not only from the fight at the hotel."

He winced. He was going to have to tell her the truth.

All of it.

His head was still fuzzy from the drugs but clear enough to know that the repercussions from this conversation would be ugly. He had to tell her not only about his current mission, but what had been happening for the past couple of years as well.

And then he'd be one more person who'd betrayed her trust. All the soft smiles she'd been sharing with him would be gone, and he wouldn't blame her for a second.

"Will you answer me something first?" He needed to know. "Why were you at the hotel?"

She looked a little embarrassed. "I was going to ask you something."

"Yeah? What's that?"

"It's not important." She reached over to the nightstand, grabbed the glass of water, and handed it to him. "You should drink. It'll help flush the drugs out of your system."

He took the water. Her evasion meant whatever she had been going to ask him was personal.

When he finished, he put down the glass. "How did you know I was in trouble?"

"I texted you, but you didn't answer so I went inside. There were three guys in the lobby who caught my attention —definitely out of place. I asked the front desk about you by name and the guys nearly fell over themselves to eavesdrop."

She began to pace. "I didn't know what was happening. I thought I might have blown some sort of cover for you or something. I ducked into a stairwell and planned to sneak out and let you know there was trouble. But then I heard the fight."

Wyatt shifted to ease the ache in his ribs. "Wasn't much of a fight, more like an ass kicking."

She shrugged. "I realized it was you, so I came to help. Pepper spray. Palm to the nose. Got you to my car and came back here."

Damn. She made it sound like it had been a trip to the grocery store rather than facing down someone who would've enjoyed doing horrible things to her. She could've *died*.

He reached out and grabbed her hand, stopping her movements as she paced. "You saved my life."

"I don't know that it was that dramatic."

"I do. Believe me, I'd be dead or wishing I was by now if you hadn't come along with your pepper spray and self-defense training."

He stood slowly, carefully. Everything hurt like a bitch, and he was stiff after all the sleeping, but his body followed his commands.

Nadine stood in front of him with her arms outstretched to catch him if he did a face-plant, but they dropped to her side when it became obvious he wasn't going to need assistance.

He grabbed his jeans from where they were folded at the foot of the bed and slid them on, catching her giving his body a once over before she looked away with a little flush.

"Somebody's trying to kill you?" she asked. "I assume that means you're not in town for a *meeting*?"

He grabbed his shirt and slid it on gingerly as they walked into the kitchen. He stretched as much as he could as he went, ignoring pain, concentrating on getting his muscles more limber. "I thought by not telling you the truth, I'd be keeping you out of some of the danger."

"Why were you in Idaho at all?"

"You saw the computer drive."

"Yes. It was in your jacket pocket?"

"A friend from Salt Lake City"—Wyatt felt like shit for every time he'd ever thought of Frank as less than a friend—"called Linear a few days ago. Evidently someone gave him that computer drive and told him it had information on it that would stop a human trafficking ring."

Nadine chewed her lip. "Okay."

"I was sent to meet him. Frank is—*was*—excitable and not the most trustworthy of sources, so we weren't sure exactly how seriously to take his claims."

"*Was?*"

Wyatt rubbed his forehead and eyes. "Someone killed him right in front of me, trying to get the drive back."

"I'm so sorry."

He gave her a nod. "They've been hunting me ever since. They have surveillance all over the Linear Tactical guys, so I can't make a direct call to them and evidently they have unparalleled access to satellite footage because they keep finding me."

Nadine didn't say anything, just walked to the refrigerator and pulled out the leftovers of their pasta primavera. She pointed for him to sit at the table as she warmed it up, then put it in front of him.

He took a bite, though the thought of Frank's death had stolen his appetite. He needed nourishment—energy to burn through the rest of the drugs. "Monday morning, they ran me off the road about ten miles south of here. I figured they'd think I would go toward Idaho Falls where it would be easier to hide, but I headed toward McCammon instead."

Her eyes went wide as she sat down next to him at the table. "That's crazy. And then you came into that market where I was shopping. Thank goodness I was there. God, what are the chances of that?"

The pasta tasted like sawdust in his mouth. *Shit.* "Nadine—"

"It's a miracle, plain and simple. You needed me and there I was." Her smile was so sweet and trusting it damn near broke his heart. "See? I told you."

"Told me what?"

"The universe was working in my favor. It was all meant to be."

This was it. He had two choices—keep lying, use her as an asset, and end any chance of a relationship, or he could tell her the truth, the whole truth.

And probably still end any chance of a relationship.

He had to try. He'd wanted her too badly for too long— and respected her too fucking much—to keep lying to her.

"Nadine." He put his fork down and covered her hand with his. "I knew you were going to be at the market. That's why I went there. It wasn't the universe; it was surveillance."

Watching the smile fall from her face ripped his guts out. Her hand slid away from his, inch by inch. "Surveillance? I don't understand . . ."

Wyatt took a deep breath. "I've been running security surveillance on you since you moved to Idaho."

"What?" She bolted up from the table. "Why? Why would you do that?"

He reached a hand toward her, but she stepped back. "Chloe was worried about you. She asked Shane to find someone who could make sure you were safe. That you were okay. Shane asked me since I'd already met you." *And was already half in love with you.* "You were all the way out here by yourself. Everything that happened had been so public. They wanted to make sure you were safe."

She looked at him with something akin to horror in her eyes. "And you?"

"I wanted to know you were safe too. You'd been through

so much already. We weren't sure if Oakley had some friends who would come after you. I didn't want you to get hurt again."

Wyatt had long since accepted that Chloe's request for help with Nadine's safety had allowed him to do what he'd desperately desired to do from the beginning: protect Nadine.

Nadine started to pace. "And what did this surveillance involve? Cameras? Have you been recording me?"

"No, nothing like that." He shook his head. "There's nothing inside the house that infringes on your privacy. My team and I did sweeps of the surrounding area to make sure no one else was keeping tabs on you. It helped that you rarely left the house."

She flinched.

Damn it. He was making this worse. "But not leaving the house much meant having more frequent deliveries. We vetted the companies you ordered from, made sure their delivery people were legit. Nothing suspicious. That sort of thing."

She stared at him and swallowed several times, then began to pace again. She was struggling, and he didn't blame her. It was a lot to work through.

"I'm so pathetic." She looked at the floor, arms wrapped around herself. Her body seemed to turn in on itself like she was trying to make herself smaller. As small as he'd made her feel.

He was out of his chair in an instant, longing to put his arms around her, dying inside because he knew that wasn't an option. Might *never* be an option again. "You aren't pathetic. Don't say that."

A snort. "Right. You've been watching me for more than two years, and I had no idea. I thought you didn't know what town I lived in! If that's not pathetic, I don't know what is.

And that stuff I was saying about the universe? What a joke."

"Can I tell you how I see it?" He laid a hand on her shoulder, relieved when she didn't pull away.

"I'm not sure if I want to hear it."

He was going to tell her anyway. He had to try. "I loved looking after you all this time."

She rolled her eyes but still didn't pull away. "Right."

"If you want to talk about pathetic, then let's talk about the fact that I was glad Shane and Chloe asked me to head your security detail. More than glad . . . *thrilled*. It gave me the excuse to see you as much as I wanted. To know you were safe, that no one was able to hurt you. Combined with the emails and messages we exchanged, it made me feel like I was truly a part of your life. It meant the world to me."

She stared at him like she still wasn't sure whether she could trust him.

"That's how I knew you would be at the market on Monday. You go every week. It's been my favorite day of the week for months."

"Why?"

"The market has some security cameras, and we hacked into them. Most of the security we've done for you has been external—not watching you, but monitoring anyone who would come in contact with you. But not the market. Because of the cameras, I could see you every Monday. Could see you walk through and pick your lovely flowers and all your fruits and vegetables."

"You watched me?"

"Every Monday. I had a damn app made so I could watch the footage on my phone no matter where I was in the world. I never missed a week. So if we're going to talk about pathetic, I think we should start with me."

Chapter 9

He'd *watched* her.

Her face was hot. She could feel it in her eyelids every time she blinked. The emotions coursed through her too quickly for her to get a handle on them. Embarrassment? Rage?

And under it all . . . *pleasure?*

He'd watched her every week for more than two years. Set it up so he could watch her from anywhere in the world.

"You think I'm a stalker, don't you?" His voice was hesitant, his hand still on her shoulder, although she had no doubt it would fall away at the slightest pull from her.

"No. Setting up security for me sounds exactly like Chloe, so I'm not surprised."

No wonder Chloe had gotten so quiet and weird on the phone whenever they talked about Wyatt. Chloe had known how much Wyatt already knew about her. Might've known he watched her each week at the Fresh Market.

She and Chloe would definitely have some words soon.

But that part about the market, was that true or was he just telling her that to make her feel better?

Now she stepped back from Wyatt's hand on her shoulder. "You know you don't have to lie to me. Not about the security—I know you're telling the truth about that. But you don't have to lie about seeing me on the market security footage being the best part of your week."

"Why would I lie about that?"

She looked down at her feet. "To make it all easier to swallow. To make me think you care about me more than you actually do." She looked up at him. "To make it so I'll help you in this situation you're in now."

He gave a brief nod. "Concern that you're being manipulated, given everything I've told you, is more than fair. But I'm not lying. If anything, if I were going to lie, it would be smarter for me *not* to have mentioned that."

Maybe. But, God, she'd been such an idiot, going on and on about how the universe had thrown them together.

She shook her head and turned to the cupboards. It was midnight, but she still filled the teakettle, set it on the stove to boil, and stared at the wall as she waited.

She had no idea what she was supposed to think or feel.

"Nadine . . ." His voice came from a few steps behind her. "Talk to me."

"You have to think I'm a moron. You have to." How could he not? "That I didn't learn anything at all by what had happened with Travis. He used me to try to kidnap and kill my best friend, and I was too stupid to see it. And I was just as trusting with you."

"It's not like that—"

"Isn't it? I know you don't want to do anything bad to me, but I'm still as gullible and trusting as I was two years ago. I still gobble up any attention any man gives to me, no matter what lies he tells. I'm like a pathetic lapdog."

The kettle screamed the way she wanted to. She'd barely

gotten it over to a different burner before Wyatt had both hands on her shoulders, turning her toward him.

"No. Stop. I'm not going to stand by while you say that ridiculous shit about yourself. If you want to be angry because I brought danger right to your doorstep, that's fine. Let me have it. You could've gotten seriously hurt, or worse, at that hotel yesterday. But you will not talk yourself down in that way. Not in front of me."

She could feel the strength of his fingers in her shoulders. They matched the intensity of his words.

Intensity about his feelings for *her*.

But could she really believe him? "Were the emails all this time part of the security? Was it because Chloe hired you? Sympathetic words to help me get through all this?"

He made a strangled sort of noise. "No, our communication had nothing to do with the security detail. I would've been messaging you as often as possible even if I had no professional reason to be near you."

She nodded and he let her go so she could turn and pour the water into her mug. It all sounded good. But, God. She still wasn't sure.

"I volunteered for your security detail. Shane contacted Zac to see who at Linear was available. As soon as I heard, I volunteered. *I* wanted to be the one to keep you safe. There was no way in hell I was leaving that to someone else."

He paced to the other side of the kitchen. She'd never seen him look so frustrated.

"I've kept my distance for more than *two years*. I wanted to ask you out. I wanted to come here and take you wherever you wanted to go for a date, but I couldn't. You weren't ready."

"I—"

"And that was fine. I wanted you to take as much time as you needed to. Like I said, there's no timetable for the speed at which someone is supposed to recover from trauma. It takes however long it takes."

He walked back and put his hands on her shoulders again. "And I was willing to wait for however long you needed. I still am, although these assholes have forced my hand. But don't you dare doubt that you've been in my thoughts every damn day because that's the absolute, honest truth."

Her eyes grew round. There could be no doubting the sincerity of his words.

He let her go and took a step back, rubbing the back of his neck, bowing his head a little. "God, I sound more like a stalker with every word I say, don't I? I'm trying to make things better, and I'm only making them worse."

"You're not making things worse."

He glanced at her, brown eyes hopeful. "I'm not?"

"It's actually sort of nice, knowing that you wanted to focus your attention on me. I mean, let's look at my history. My last boyfriend used me to get information about my best friend before he kidnapped her. Hell, my own mother didn't care enough about me to get off drugs. That's how I met Chloe in the foster system. So, it's a pleasant change, knowing somebody was looking out for me."

He tilted his head to the side as he studied her. "You know what I would like? To take you to Oak Creek sometime to meet my brothers, the Linear Tactical guys. That's what they are to me, my brothers, in every way but blood. I want to introduce you to my family too, but it would mean just as much to me to introduce you to my team."

She stiffened and set her mug down on the counter. "Wyatt, you really don't need to sweet-talk me. Thank you for looking out for my safety, but I release you from that. I'll have a talk with Chloe and Shane and make sure they know the security detail needs to end. I'll still help you with whatever is going on now. I'm assuming you need to get to Oak Creek?"

He ran a hand through his thick brown hair. "Yes, I do. And it's going to be tricky."

"I know you'll figure it out," she said softly. "I don't want you to think you have to be nice to me to get me to help you—"

He grabbed her by the waist and pulled her close, his face mere inches from hers. "I'm not sweet-talking you or letting you down easy. Yes, please and thank you, I need your help. But what I'm saying to you is not about that. I've wanted to take you to meet my Linear Tactical family for a long time, but I wanted you to be ready first."

"Oh."

He growled softly. "You're allowed to be mad at me for how I've handled this. I fucked up, and I'm sorry."

She squeaked as he pulled her closer, every inch of his hard muscled body against her much softer curves.

"What you aren't allowed to do," he continued in a deeper voice than before, "is think I don't want you. *Nothing* could be further from the truth."

Her heart pounded against her ribs almost painfully. "Really?" she whispered, almost afraid to hope it was true.

"Really. You're the only thing I've been able to think about for two years. I haven't been so much as interested in dating anyone else. You've been on my mind ever since I met you in the hospital. You were so brave and strong, even in the middle of everything. I couldn't forget you."

His touch was real. His nearness was real. Why couldn't she get out of her own way and accept what he said as the truth? Why was she so reluctant to believe him?

Maybe it was all wrong and would ruin the moment, but she had to know.

"How can you feel that way after knowing how stupid

and gullible I was with Travis? I let him use me. I was blind for ages. And then, because I was too stupid to see who he was, somebody I loved ended up in danger. How can you look at me and know that and mean anything you've said?"

His thumb and finger hooked under her chin, lifting her face to him. "You're a trusting person. That's not the same as being stupid or gullible. You want to believe the best in people because you have an amazing heart. That's something I've learned about you as we've talked, a little bit more with every message, and I'm so glad I did."

His lips were gentle as they moved against hers, like she was treasured. Like he wanted to take his time and explore all the nuances of her mouth. He licked and nipped at her lower lip ever so softly.

She sighed and parted her lips as his tongue probed, deepening their connection. His hands slid up her back and down again, settling on her hips. She froze for a second at his touch. Her hips—their width—weren't exactly her favorite body part.

He didn't shy away or move back up to her waist. Instead, he groaned, his fingers digging into her flesh like he wanted her more. His lips got harder, more possessive.

Nadine let herself melt into it. Melt into *him*. But God, she needed to be careful, his body was still recovering from the multiple injuries he'd sustained over the past few days.

"I don't want to hurt you," she breathed between kisses as he nipped her chin, jawline, and earlobe. What she wanted more than anything was to indulge in touching him, exploring his chiseled body, but the memory of those bruises made her hold back.

"Believe me, you couldn't," he whispered before covering her mouth again, thrusting his tongue inside, demanding more. He lifted her, making her squeal in surprise before settling her onto the counter.

He'd lifted her like she weighed nothing.

She wrapped her legs around him, drawing him closer. She'd dreamed of this, of *him*, and he was finally in her arms.

He trailed kisses down her chin and throat. She let her head fall back, eyes closed, a sigh escaping.

"So sweet," he groaned against her skin, raining kisses along her collarbone. She threaded her fingers through his thick hair, holding his head close, tightening her legs around his waist.

What meant more than anything, more than the physical pleasure threatening to undo her, was the deep satisfaction of knowing this was real. Wyatt wanted her.

This incredible man stood head and shoulders above any man she'd ever so much as spoken to. He was so brave, so strong, so fierce and loyal.

He thought she was worth the trouble of looking after for years.

He thought she was beautiful. He saw her heart and appreciated it.

He saw *her*.

A knot of need twisted inside as she wrapped her arms around his neck and pressed her lips back to his. There was nowhere in the world she'd rather be than here with him.

Chapter 10

His years as a Green Beret had taught Wyatt patience and that the most rewarding things in life were almost always products of delayed gratification.

Kissing Nadine was so damned worth the wait.

Two years' worth of fantasies flowed between them with each nip of their teeth or playful duel of their tongues.

Each groan. Moan. Sigh.

There was nothing he wanted more than to continue until they both forgot their names—which at this rate probably wouldn't take more than a few minutes.

But instead, he reached for the control he so prided himself on and reeled himself in.

It was one of the hardest things he'd ever done. But damn it, he'd been unconscious for more than twenty-four hours, and on the run for three days before that. He needed to get this computer drive into the right hands. Lives were at stake.

But Nadine was sitting on the counter, breathless. She was wide-eyed in the dim kitchen light, face flushed, lips swollen and red. He couldn't tear his eyes away.

He trailed his thumbs across her cheek. "You're beautiful and there's nothing more I want to do than to drag you back to the bedroom."

"I don't think I would argue with that."

A groan fell from his lips and he slid his forehead against hers. "I need to take care of this situation with the computer drive first. It's the life-or-death sort of important. I've already been out of it for too long."

She took a breath and nodded. "How can I help?"

He cupped her cheeks and kissed her gently before helping her down from the counter. He wasn't sure there was anything sexier than a woman who worked the problem.

She grabbed his half-eaten plate of pasta and popped it back into the microwave.

"I'm not exactly sure who is after me, but they've already proven they're willing to kill to get the drive. At this point, I think the only reason I'm still alive is because they want to question me." And by question, he meant torture until he wished for death. "They don't know if I've hidden it or sent it to someone."

She took out the plate and handed it to him. "Eat." She pointed to the table.

He smiled and sat down at the table. "Yes, ma'am." It was nice to have someone looking after him.

"Do we need to mail the drive somewhere?"

"It's too important to take a chance on the mail, not to mention might get a poor mailman killed. I need to hand deliver it to my friend Kendrick Foster, Linear's computer expert." He took a bite. "I texted him when I first woke up."

"Can they trace your phone? I powered it off because I thought they might be able to track you."

So brilliant. He smiled at her. "Smart, but that's not my real phone. I had to get rid of it almost immediately. The one I have now is a burner, a throwaway phone. There is no way to trace it to me."

"So the bad guys don't know you're here?"

"They shouldn't. I was careful to keep you out of this." He shot her a half smile and shook his head. "They didn't know you existed until you came into the hotel like the cavalry."

She raised an eyebrow. "Lucky for you I did."

"Sweetheart, you are all sorts of lucky for me. The hotel was only the most recent part of that."

He loved the little flush that tinged her cheeks. She pointed at his plate. "I don't have any more pasta, but I'm going to make myself an omelet. Want some protein?"

"I definitely wouldn't say no."

And now the part he knew was coming that he hadn't been looking forward to. He gritted his teeth. "I was wondering if I could borrow your car. I've got to get to Oak Creek."

"I thought you said they'd be waiting for you there. That they were watching."

"I'll have to figure that out when I get there."

She turned and started cracking eggs for the omelets. "You said they don't know about me. What if I come with you and deliver the computer drive under the guise of something else?"

God, that would make his life so much easier. But still . . . "I don't want to drag you into anything dangerous. These people chasing me are unusually well-connected."

"But they're looking for a man traveling alone, right? Having me with you would throw them off."

"I can't ask you to do that."

She turned around, spatula in hand. "You're not asking. I'm offering."

He closed the distance between them, leaning against the counter. "I want to keep you safe."

She turned back to the eggs but glanced over at him. "I think I've been trying to keep myself safe also. Too safe. Maybe it's time I start trying to find the person I was—the person I know I can be—instead."

There wasn't much argument he could make against that now, was there?

He reached for her and slid his hand around the back of her head so he could kiss the spot below her ear. "Then I will gladly accept your offer to escort me to Oak Creek. Looks like I'll get to introduce you to my family there sooner than I thought."

She leaned her head into him. "Okay, good. I want to help."

"You already have. But I'm sure you will some more." He kissed her jaw again, then took the plate with the omelet she offered. They sat back down to eat together.

It was after midnight, and they should get going soon, using the cover of night to their advantage. But when they'd finished eating and she walked by him with her plate, he couldn't resist pulling her into his lap.

"Another kiss," he murmured. "I know we have to go but I want another kiss."

He wanted so much more than that. He ached for more as their lips met, melded, and heat singed them both. For the first time in his life, he was about to put his own desires above the importance of a mission. And he wasn't going to apologize for it.

But then the kitchen window burst inward, and some sort of bottle bomb landed near the sink. It crashed into the ground. The scent of kerosene filled the room a moment before the kitchen burst into flames.

"Oh my God!" Nadine's scream rose over the rush of the rapidly spreading fire.

He set her on her feet, wrapped an arm around her waist, and pushed her toward the bedroom. "Go, go!"

Shit. They'd found him.

A second bottle bomb hurtled through the window where they'd been sitting at the table and burst on the hard floor, spreading outward.

Damn it, incendiary devices from both sides meant that the house was surrounded. There would be armed men at both the front and rear doors.

Those men were waiting until the house was engulfed. Until Wyatt and Nadine had no choice but to get out or burn to death.

Nadine clung to him as he cut them to the right, backtracking once again toward the bedroom. She had to be suffering flashbacks from the fire that had burned her, but she was holding it together.

He shielded her, getting her to the bedroom. "Get dressed." It came out as a bark, but there was no time to be gentle. "Dark colors. Black, if you can."

"What are we going to do?"

"I hate to tell you this, sweetheart, but I'm going to have to make things worse."

She pulled on black yoga pants. "How?"

He shoved his feet into his boots and then his jacket, stuffing the drive into the pocket. He left the burner phone—somehow they must have tracked him through it. "Do you have liquor in the house?"

"Yes. Why?"

"I'm going to need to set the rest of your house on fire."

"What? Why would—"

"To confuse them. Either we confuse them by spreading

the fire so they don't know which way we'll try to escape, or we run straight into them."

Which would lead to a very painful death.

He cupped her face for a brief second. "I'm sorry."

Sorry that she had to face fire again. Sorry he was about to burn down the nest she'd built for herself.

"It's okay." But her face was pale as she bent down to tie her shoes.

She was struggling, fingers shaking, so he crouched in front of her and tied the other one, then helped her to her feet.

"Come on. We'll go through the spare bedroom window on the other side of the house. Hurry."

He rigged two more bombs using bottles from the small bar. "Go to the spare room," he ordered. "Leave the lights out and stay away from the window. I'll meet you in there."

He went to her bedroom and couldn't help but think of what they could've been doing. Instead of throwing Nadine onto the bed, he threw a bottle bomb at the wall under the window and let it smash, spreading fire onto the curtains.

The second bottle followed the first, sending a ball of fire out a different window. That would definitely get the attention of the people waiting outside.

Meanwhile, he'd be on the other side of the house, climbing out a window.

Nadine was there, waiting for him, holding her shirt over her mouth and nose. Smoke was starting to spread through the entire single-floor structure. She was still holding it together. She truly didn't give herself enough credit.

He grabbed her hand. "Come on. Through the window. As soon as we're out, as fast as you can into the woods."

The woods and wilderness would be to his advantage—SERE training in real life. He kept her along the wall next to the window, out of sight, while he listened for anyone who might be waiting nearby. It sounded like the flames coming from Nadine's room had drawn everybody's attention, which was what he'd counted on.

"Let's go. Quiet as possible." He opened the window and climbed out, then helped her to the ground. Hand in hand, they ran for the woods.

They hadn't made it far before someone spotted them. "They're out here, around the side!"

Wyatt didn't slow down at the voice calling out behind them, but prayed bullets wouldn't follow. He sprinted for the cover of the tall, sprawling trees a few hundred feet ahead, his hand around hers in an iron grip. She ran silently next to him.

There was a better chance of hiding once they crossed the tree line—but at least three men were hot on their heels. All of Wyatt's quasi-stalkerish behavior would come in handy now—he had studied these woods in case he ever found himself in them.

This wasn't what he'd had in mind.

They ran hard for long minutes. Nadine struggled to keep up. She didn't complain, but he knew she couldn't keep this pace much longer.

There was a ravine up ahead, deep and crisscrossed with the exposed roots of the gnarled trees that lined both banks. Moonlight was all he had to go by as he led Nadine in that direction.

"This way," he whispered over his shoulder. "We'll hide down there."

He helped her down the root-covered slope but hesitated, listening for the men pursuing them. They didn't have the advantage of knowing the area, but they were faster runners.

"Where are they?" She was still trying to catch her breath as he helped her lower. In her black clothes, she blended with their surroundings pretty well, so long as she kept her face down and out of the moonlight.

He listened again, able to tell the general location by the sounds—and lack thereof—in the forest around them.

"I think they spread out a little and they're not bothering to try to be quiet." Sure enough, within seconds he heard voices carrying their way.

He held her tight. She was trembling, her heart pounding hard enough for him to feel it under his arm. "It'll be okay," he whispered in her ear, staring up at the banks.

"Check in the trees too," one of the men called out. "He's a slick one, or at least, he thinks he is."

"Guess his girlfriend won't like that he burned her place down," a second man replied. The others laughed, a cold, nasty sound.

He pulled her closer, wishing he could apologize.

"Not your fault," she whispered before ducking her head, hiding her face in his neck. This woman trusted him, and he wouldn't let her down.

He'd spent the past two years making sure she was safe from a distance. Now he was going to do it up close.

The beam of a flashlight broke over the bank. Wyatt lowered his head, staying as still as he could. In the middle of so many roots, many of which rose higher than him and Nadine, it would take an eagle eye to spot them.

"Lexington! What've you got?"

The man who spoke up was close enough to make Nadine jump. Wyatt held her tighter, closer, shielding her with his body. If they wanted to get to her, they'd have to go through him.

"Nothing yet. But the longer that bastard makes me look for him, the more fun it'll be when I catch him and force him to talk. What I did to him at the hotel will look like a warm-up."

Lexington was the one nearby holding the flashlight whose beam swept back and forth across the banks of the ravine. "And now I'll get to play with the woman, too . . . which will make it twice as fun."

He was trying to scare them, trying to get them to panic and make some sort of break for it. Nadine whimpered softly against his neck, and he threaded his fingers in her hair, holding her firm against him.

The flashlight beam swept the roots lining the ravine. Wyatt ducked his head not a second before the light washed over them. He held Nadine tight enough that he was sure he had to be hurting her, but she didn't so much as flinch.

"I can hardly wait to get to know her up close and personal." Lexington snickered. "I'll make him watch as I play with her. See if that loosens his tongue any quicker. Getting the hard drive location is the job, but slicing up the two of them will be my pleasure."

Wyatt waited, motionless, as the beam moved farther down the ravine, and the direction of Lexington's footfalls followed suit.

Then, he waited some more.

He could feel Nadine tense. She obviously didn't understand why they weren't moving if Lexington and his friends were gone.

Still, Wyatt waited. They'd called him *Scout* for a reason in the Special Forces. He was patient, willing to outwait whatever he needed to. Usually it was his prey, but in this case he was outwaiting the hunter.

It was long—so very long—and Wyatt began to doubt his own instincts. Nadine, to her credit, remained silent and still, pressed against him the whole time. That sort of stillness took a toll, mentally and physically.

Then finally.

"Come on, Lexington, they're gone for Christ's sake. Nobody would sit around and wait this long."

Nadine let out a silent gasp against his neck. Wyatt's instincts had been right. Lexington and his men had been waiting for them. If he and Nadine had moved, they'd have been caught.

"Fuck," Lexington said. "I was sure they were around here. I guess they crossed the river somewhere else."

"We need to call in and get some more people out here to help look for them. Get more people on Oak Creek too."

"Yeah." Frustration and anger dripped from Lexington's words. "But make sure everyone knows they have to be taken alive and that Highfield is mine. He's going to regret making me chase him through the fucking wilderness."

They left, for real this time, still talking as they went.

"They're gone," he whispered in Nadine's ear. "Come on. We've got to go deeper into the woods."

Nadine took his hand and he helped her to her feet. He climbed up the other side of the ravine with Nadine following close behind.

He knew where he wanted to head: where the river split a couple of miles away. When thunder rumbled in the distance, he smiled.

"Perfect. A storm's coming."

"A storm is perfect? I'm afraid to ask why."

Once they got on relatively level terrain, they set off at a brisk jog. "Because it's going to make everything unbearably miserable."

Chapter 11

Unbearably miserable. Wasn't that what Wyatt had said?

He'd definitely gotten that right.

How many miles had they run? Five? Ten? A hundred?

One foot in front of the other. That was all Nadine could think about. All she could do. That was what her life had boiled down to while Wyatt led her step after step through the wilderness.

She wasn't going to slow them down. She *couldn't* slow them down. If she did, Lexington would kill them both in horrible ways. So, she kept going.

She put one foot in front of the other when it began to rain.

She put one foot in front of the other when her shoes began to rub blisters on her heels and every muscle in her body screamed for her to stop.

She turned her mind off and kept her body on autopilot —the same way she'd done for weeks after what had happened with Travis. Finally, some damned good was coming out of the inescapable numbness she'd found herself trapped in for so long. She would ignore everything else and focus on putting one foot in front of the other.

She had no idea where they were, and her system had long since burned through any calories it had. Her entire body cried out for rest, but she refused to voice any of her needs.

Wyatt was trying to put as much distance between them and Lexington's vile threats as possible. The least she could do was not be a baby.

One foot in front of the other.

It wasn't until she ran into Wyatt's back that she realized he'd stopped. He was quick, grabbing her with one arm before she could fall. Good thing, because she didn't know if she'd be able to get back up if she fell to the ground.

"Look at me." She couldn't figure out how to do what he asked, so he tipped her chin upward with one finger. "You're done. It's time to stop. You've had enough."

"No, no. I can keep going." She meant it with all her heart, but she could hear the exhaustion in her voice.

And now that they had stopped moving, she started to shake uncontrollably.

She tried to stop it, tried to force herself to stay in control. But her body had had enough. Her mind wasn't far behind.

He muttered a curse and slid an arm around her. "I'm sorry. I should've slowed down long before now. You're too much of a damn trouper for your own good."

"I-I know we have to keep going. Lexington—"

Wyatt wiped hair off her brow, sliding it back from her eyes. She'd run out of energy to do that hours ago.

"Lexington and his men are nowhere nearby." He cursed again as he looked in her eyes, both drenched by the constant rain. "I'm a fucking idiot, sweetheart. I'm so sorry."

"I-I'm okay." Admitting the truth wasn't going to help.

"You were up all night taking care of me, and now this . . . We're going to stop and rest for a few hours. I can guarantee they are nowhere near us."

"Where can we go?"

"Let's do some real-life SERE training." He kept her tucked against his side as they moved forward, following a small river they'd come to earlier. The soft whooshing sound of the water as it flowed past would've been soothing under different circumstances.

Where the hell were they? Letting Wyatt lead her, she looked around but couldn't make heads or tails of anything. He definitely didn't have the same problem, sure-footed and confident. She leaned on his strength as he led them away.

It was so good to have someone's strength to lean on.

They walked for another few minutes in silence before he stopped and pointed up ahead where a steep cliffside loomed high enough to make her crane her neck to take it all in.

He didn't mean they had to climb that, did he? Her legs were so weak she could barely stand on her own. She doubted she could've climbed it in daylight at full strength, and she knew she definitely could not climb it now.

"There should be some sort of overhang near the base," he explained. "Not quite a cave, but deep enough that we can take shelter there. We have landscapes like this all over the place near Oak Creek. There's almost always an overhang."

The thunder rumbled louder, and the wind picked up, urging them to rush forward. Knowing there was a place to rest ahead made it easier. Almost.

The shallow cave wasn't much, but it was dry. Wyatt checked for any critters, then helped her inside.

"I'd build a fire—show you some real SERE techniques —but we can't risk detection."

"It's okay." The early fall air wasn't too bad now that the rain wasn't pelting them.

But with the lack of physical agony, all the mental ones came pouring back. Ones she hadn't allowed herself to think about at all while they'd rushed through the wilderness.

The house, her haven, her safe place. It was gone, burned to the ground. The rain would've been too late to save it from destruction.

She tried to push the thoughts away before they overtook her, but it was no use. Now that they'd stopped moving and it was time to rest, there was no escaping what she'd left behind.

It was all gone.

They could have died earlier. What if the men had charged into the house and shot them? What if Lexington had had his way and tortured her while Wyatt had been forced to watch?

Where would she go after this? How could she hope to rebuild her life from scratch again?

She sank to the cold, stone ground with her back against the rock wall. Her hands shook, so she pressed them together and held them between her knees so Wyatt wouldn't see.

He had enough to deal with. She didn't need to add her breakdown to that list.

He was setting up some sort of branch barricade at the front of their small cave to protect them. Maybe he wouldn't notice she was falling apart.

But when he looked back at her, he knew. She didn't know how, but he knew.

Once he was done with the barricade, he crawled to where she'd balled into herself.

"Hey," he whispered.

"I-I . . ." She couldn't seem to find any words.

"It's okay." He sat next to her, shoulder to shoulder. "It's okay to feel whatever it is you're feeling. You've been so focused, so brave. You don't have to be brave right now."

A crack of thunder and suddenly, the storm broke harder than it had when they'd been out in it.

Like the sky was sobbing.

Nadine found herself sobbing too. All the fear and anger and despair flowed out of her in waves of pain she couldn't control. She had no idea how long it lasted and barely felt it when Wyatt pulled her into his lap.

He didn't try to quiet her. Didn't offer her meaningless words of comfort. Didn't try to fix it.

He just held her and lent her his strength.

Nobody had ever done that for her. Chloe had tried as her friend, but she'd always had her own demons to fight.

Wyatt held her and let his strength surround them both like the solid, immoveable calm in her raging storm.

Eventually her tears passed. "I'm sorry for getting so—"

"No," he cut her off before she could finish the sentence. "You don't apologize. I've seen trained soldiers lose their shit over less than what you've been through in the past couple days."

She nodded against his chest. "Thank you for letting me get it out. I wouldn't have made it if it weren't for you."

He gave a short bark of laughter that held no humor. "Yeah. And if it weren't for me, you'd still have a house. And no psychopaths chasing you through the wilderness threatening to torture you. I never should've brought you into this. I'm so sor—"

"No. Now _you_ don't apologize." She was as stern as he'd been. She turned in his lap and grabbed the collar of his jacket, pulling him close. "If you hadn't come to me, you might be dead by now. I can't stand to think about it."

"But you lost everything because of me."

"I lost _stuff_ because said psychopaths decided to destroy

my house. All of that is replaceable. *You* got us out. *You* kept us safe. That's the most important thing."

She hadn't planned to kiss him but couldn't keep her lips from his. Then, they couldn't stop. She kissed him like he was oxygen and she was out of air, breathing him in over and over. At least part of it was the adrenaline from the night, from her outburst, but she didn't care.

Knowing they'd come so close to dying multiple times during the past few hours deepened her need to be close to him, to indulge in him, to soak in every minute of this intimate togetherness.

She didn't care if they were in some sort of cave. Didn't care if he had said he wanted to wait until they had uninterrupted time to enjoy each other.

Uninterrupted time was a luxury they might never have. She wanted him. And the deep moan that escaped his throat let her know how much he wanted her too.

His hands slid up under her shirt, stroking bare skin, heating her blood. She needed to be closer, needed to feel his skin against hers.

He pulled back when she lifted her shirt over her head. "Are you sure? We can wait."

"I'm surer than I've been about anything in a long time." She could barely make out his features in their enclosure. She used her fingers to trace the lines of his face. "I want you, Wyatt. Here. Please."

He turned his face to kiss one of her palms, then the other. "You don't have to ask me twice, sweetheart, believe me." He pulled his shirt off, which joined her clothes in a pile.

Straddling him, she lowered herself until their chests were touching and kissed him again while his hands traced her hips, her thighs, her back.

She shuddered as his lips left hers and made their way

down her throat, then nibbled on her shoulder. One hand buried in her hair and the other gripped her hip. He pulled her down while pushing upward.

The friction of their bodies grinding together had them both groaning. Yes, she definitely wanted him.

They shifted away long enough to strip away the rest of their clothing. His teasing lips and teeth found her breasts— nipping, soothing, driving her crazy—when he was quicker than her in pulling down his jeans.

While she tried to get her pants off, his lips tormented her nipple. "You better hurry."

"No fair. You barely pulled your pants down at all." Her head fell back with a moan as he took her breast deep into his mouth, sucking hard. "I have to take mine all the way off."

"Gives me more time to enjoy these." He switched to the other breast, giving it the same treatment. "You're so damn sexy, Nadine."

"How do you know? You can't see me."

"I don't have to see you to know you're sexy. Everything about you—your strength, your courage, your beauty—is damn near perfect." He reached up to cup her neck and pulled her forehead down to his. "When this is over, we're going to do this somewhere safe and soft, where we have a long, long time for me to drive you crazy."

"Promise?"

"Scout's honor."

"Your code name."

He nodded. "And this time, the most solemn of promises."

"Deal."

He dug into his pocket and pulled out a condom. "I wasn't expecting this sort of adventure, so all I have is the one in my wallet."

She scooted back and watched as he opened the package and slid the condom over his hard length. She wanted him inside her. *Now*. It was an actual ache.

Thunder crashed overhead.

"I need you," she whispered. "As wild and brutal as that storm outside, I need you to remind me that we're both still alive and that's something not to take for granted. We'll have slow and easy another time, but right now, all I want is you inside me."

He grunted, obviously pleased with her words. She pushed at his shoulders until he was lying back, then climbed on top of him.

"You go as fast or slow as you need, sweetheart," he whispered. "I'm all yours."

She bit her lip, slowly working herself on him. It had been so long, and it felt so good. He held still, letting her control the pace and depth, but she could feel his fingers bite into her hips and ass.

And she loved it.

She cried out softly when she took him as deep as he would go. His head tilted back as he let out a groan, tremors racking him as he attempted to hold still.

For her. For her to find *her* pleasure.

She raised herself slowly, feeling every inch of him, then lowered. Taking her time, wanting to savor this one moment.

He reached up, taking her breasts in his palms. She whimpered when his thumbs stroked back and forth across her erect nipples. The touch sent bolts of electricity straight to her core. She moved faster, grinding against him on the downstroke, doubling her pleasure.

"So beautiful," he groaned. "You're always so beautiful."

All of it—wanting him, needing him, the fear, the pain, the knowledge of him watching her for the past years, the sheer joy of being with him this way, the heat unspooling in her core—came together at once. She was lost, head thrown back, crying out with every breath as her climax came faster than she had expected.

Distantly she heard him call out her name as his hips pumped beneath her. She fell against his chest.

The storm raged around them as he held her against his heart.

Chapter 12

Note to self: carry more than one condom in case of emergency entrapment in a cave with a gorgeous woman.

Lying there with Nadine in his arms, Wyatt smiled in the darkness as he stroked her hair. They were both too exhausted to put more condoms to good use anyway.

And happy. In spite of everything, he was happier than he'd been in a long time.

He'd already known she was amazing. Brave, beautiful, giving.

What he hadn't known was how tough she was. He'd set a pace that would've made trained soldiers balk, leading her over uneven terrain, up steep inclines, never slowing for fear of being caught.

And she'd kept up, never once complained, never once asked him to slow down.

He'd wanted to kick his own ass when he'd stopped and seen her complete and utter exhaustion. *Another note to self: Nadine needs someone who will put her well-being at the forefront.*

He'd be more than happy to volunteer for that position.

Now she slept like the dead, wrapped up against him.

She deserved it. They'd both gotten their clothes back on after their lovemaking in case they needed to leave quickly, but then he'd told her to sleep.

Wyatt wanted to hold her, let her rest, protect her. If it weren't for the danger stalking them—and lack of condoms —he'd be tempted to stay here much longer.

Once he got this drive delivered and neutralized the threat to her, he planned to drag Nadine to the nearest bed. It might take two or three years to really get to know every inch of her, but that would be okay.

It might take forever. And that would be even better.

He waited for any tinge of panic at the thought, but the truth was he'd known Nadine was the sort of forever he wanted from the moment he'd first met her in that hospital more than two years ago. Getting to know her since had only reaffirmed what his heart had known from the first moment.

She was it for him.

And now that there were no more secrets between them, he needed to convince her of that too. And make sure she was ready to move forward.

But first, safety.

She stirred, her head rubbing along his chest. She didn't seem in a hurry to wake up. He didn't blame her, but they had to.

"I hate to wake you," he nuzzled the top of her head, "but we need to get moving."

When she angled her face toward his, he kissed her lips and knew it was something he planned to do many times in the future. Every morning, every night, and as many times in between as possible.

Rather than loosening, her arm tightened around his waist. "Can't we stay here?"

"It doesn't seem half bad, does it? Although I assume we'd want plumbing at some point."

They both sat up, stretching sore muscles, then walked to the shelter opening. Moving the crude doorway he'd made of bush and branches, they peered out at the early morning.

"Stay here," he murmured. "I want to double-check that no one is nearby."

He did a quick, silent loop of the surrounding area and saw nothing out of place. The creature noises around him reassured him that they didn't have any strangers in their midst. Their punishing pace yesterday had paid off.

He headed back to Nadine. Once they got going, they'd want to move briskly and take advantage of the lead they had on Lexington and his men.

He helped her out of their small shelter, and she tipped her head back to soak in the sun for a moment once she stretched fully. "At least the storm passed. I was worried we'd have to keep going in a downpour."

"Me too, to be honest. We'll have to be careful of mud and loose rock, but today should be much easier."

"We could be anywhere in the world right now when you think about it. As far as the eye can see, nothing but trees." She wrapped her arms around herself.

"But in actuality, we're about four miles northeast of the nearest town." She looked at him in surprise and he shrugged. "Stalking you for a year has come in handy. Studying the terrain was part of the job."

"So, where do we go?"

He pointed. "Southwest. If we head that way, we should end up in Downey, the next town over. This area and the river are what separate McCammon and Downey. Should take about an hour and a half since we won't be running. You up for it?"

"No running? Definitely up for it."

Wyatt wasn't surprised when they followed the river and by midmorning ended up right where he'd expected them to be, on the outskirts of Downey. They kept away from everyone else, careful not to draw attention to themselves.

"At least it's bigger than McCammon," Nadine observed.

He chuckled. "That's not saying much."

He scanned the main drag that cut through the heart of the little downtown area. There were boutiques, a bank, a few bakeries, and some coffee shops . . . and plenty of opportunities to steal a car from a parking lot.

Before he attempted that, however, he had to get something straight with Nadine.

He pulled her into a small alley so they could talk. "Before we go any further, you have a choice to make. You can either come with me or we can separate."

Her hand grabbed his. "What? I thought—"

"Hear me out. If we call Chloe, she has the resources to get help to you in a few hours. She'll make sure you're safe, either around here or you could go hang out with her and Shane for a while in North Carolina."

"Or?"

"I have a few backdoor channels I could use to get in touch with some people who could keep you protected. They can stash you in a safe house until everything is clear. Once this is over, I'll help you with finding a new place to live."

"What if I want to stay with you?"

"You can, but I'm about to steal a car." He shot her a knowing look. "I'm not on any official law enforcement business. If I get arrested, we're talking grand theft auto, to which you'd be aiding and abetting. Are you sure you want to risk that?"

Part of him wanted her to choose her own safety. But the bigger part of him wanted to keep her with him.

"I'm staying with you." She gave him a half grin. "There's no telling how many times you'll get yourself killed if I'm not around to save you."

This woman . . . Living without her was becoming less and less of an option.

He kissed her hard, then grabbed her hand and pulled her back toward the street. "Let's go, spitfire."

They walked until they came to a covered garage with nobody behind the service desk. Nadine kept a lookout while Wyatt took a set of keys from a hook and found a Honda in the spot corresponding with the hook number.

Only once they were an hour outside town did they stop for something to eat and to fill the tank. Wyatt paid with cash and kept his head down. They stopped at a supercenter thirty minutes later. Nadine went in and bought another burner phone while Wyatt took the license plate off a rundown vehicle in the back of the lot and traded it with theirs.

Hopefully, that would keep the good guys off them long enough for them to stop the bad guys.

They drove toward Oak Creek.

"I need to get the drive to Kendrick, but he's being watched. Phones bugged too since they had to have found us by the text I sent him from the burner phone. Approaching him directly isn't an option."

Nadine turned to him. "What if you stay hidden and I get the drive to him?"

"I don't like the idea of you getting so involved."

"In case you forgot, I'm already pretty deeply involved."

He blew out a long sigh. "I haven't forgotten, believe me."

"It's a good plan. You're a known employee of Linear Tactical; I'm not. They know you were with a woman, but what are the odds any of the bad guys would be able to pick me out of a crowd if you weren't with me?"

He growled, staring at the road ahead. This wasn't how he'd wanted things to go at all. As gratifying as it was to know she wanted to be with him, it would've been better for her to call Chloe and get the hell out of there.

"You know I'm right," she added after he stayed silent for too long.

"Don't rub it in."

"It'll be fine." She reached over and grabbed his hand. "I want to help. I'm happy to help. It's more than just us at stake here. You said this is going to help take down a human trafficking ring. I want to do that."

He brought her hand up to his lips and kissed it. "Thank you."

They drove for a couple more hours, then stopped a few miles outside of Oak Creek so he could lie down in the back seat while Nadine took the wheel. He video called her from the burner phone. "Hold it up, facing the windshield, propped on the wheel," he instructed. "I want to be able to see where we're headed."

She drove through town like nothing was the matter. "This place is beautiful," she whispered. "I wish we were here under different circumstances."

"Believe me, so do I." He wished they were here in any other circumstance besides putting her in possible danger again. "You'll follow this street another half mile before making a right."

She followed his instructions, and soon they were on the street where Kendrick lived. "Easy does it," he murmured, watching through the phone. "His house is on the next block, about halfway down on your left."

They were only halfway down the block when Wyatt spotted trouble. "Damn it. Keep rolling. Don't look toward the house."

"What do you see?" she asked out of the corner of her mouth.

"Two black cars with tinted windows parked across the

street. They definitely don't belong there. That's the advantage of living in a small town—you know when something's out of place."

"What should I do?"

"Keep going another mile or so before turning back toward town. Not too slow—that could draw attention."

She drove and he watched. The whole fucking town had eyes on it. Through her phone, he spotted at least half a dozen potential threats. Lexington and his cohorts were definitely counting on Wyatt contacting Kendrick or one of the other Linear guys.

"What should I do?" Nadine's voice was soft, steady, but he could tell the strain was getting to her.

"Keep rolling. I'm watching."

She drove another block, then another. There was a red light up ahead. She brought them to a stop.

"Wyatt." It was a whisper.

"Yeah?"

"There are two guys standing on the sidewalk to the right . . . they're watching the car. They're looking straight at me. I think they might have seen me when I drove through before."

Shit. Some of Lexington's guys? "Swivel the phone in their direction so I can see." Holding his breath, he watched the image change.

Finally, the men came into view and Wyatt relaxed.

"It's a green light," Nadine whispered. "Should I keep going? They're still watching me."

"No, pull into the first spot you come to and park."

"A-are you sure?"

"Definitely." She parked a few doors down from the corner. "Those two men are Zac Mackay and Finn Bollinger. I'm not surprised you seemed suspicious to them."

"Why?"

"If I had to guess, they're already aware of eyes on them from Lexington's guys. Then they see a strange vehicle cruising through town more than once? They might have noticed how you're holding your phone and recognized it as a way to feed video to another phone. They're trained to pick up on stuff civilians miss."

"Okay. They sound a little scary." She let out a long, shaky breath. "What next?"

"How would you feel about delivering a message to them?"

Chapter 13

If there was an actual, physical list of things that made Nadine uncomfortable, walking up to two gorgeous alpha males to make conversation would be at the top.

She tried to tell herself it was better than running through the wilderness or standing in her house as it caught fire or listening to what Lexington had planned to do if he caught her.

But seriously, it wasn't much better.

Wyatt's friends—who, like him, had muscles for days and probably trained like it was their full-time job—glanced at her as she walked toward them, then started talking to each other.

She knew who they were, but they didn't know who she was. Would they mock her for daring to speak to them? Were they judging her for the extra fifteen pounds she carried around her waist and hips? Would they believe her when she told them she had a message from Wyatt?

If it weren't for Wyatt, she would go back to the car and figure out another way. Every time she'd been taunted as a fat teenager came zooming to the forefront of her mind.

A sign reading *Frontier Diner* hung over the building Zac and Finn headed into before Nadine could reach them. Which of them was which? Wyatt hadn't said. All that mattered was getting his message right. Maybe she could catch them before they sat down to eat.

The second she stepped through the door of the bustling diner, her phone buzzed.

I lost you. Everything okay?

She had to smile at his protectiveness in the middle of so much anxiety. *Followed them into the diner. All good.*

She hoped. But it wasn't bad in the way Wyatt was worried about. She could do this. Wyatt needed her to do this.

And considering the condition of what used to be her house and the fact that her life was also in danger, she needed to do it for herself.

She didn't let herself hesitate, crossing to the booth where the two men sat. Their size practically overwhelmed the table between them. But where Wyatt's size made her feel feminine and beautiful, theirs was intimidating.

And they were even more handsome close-up. *Not helpful.*

They looked up at her when she reached them. *This was it.* This was when they'd wonder why a fat girl would bother to approach them.

She spoke up before they had the chance. "Excuse me. Um . . . Cyclone and Eagle?"

She expected snickers or straight-up mockery, but instead, they both sat up a little straighter.

"Yes," the darker one with green eyes said.

"I have a message for you." Her eyes slid to each side, making sure nobody around was listening before she lowered her volume. "Um, from Scout."

They recognized the name instantly. The man to her right moved over to give her room. "Please. Sit."

She sat down at the end of the booth beside him, took a deep breath and recited what Wyatt had made her repeat a dozen times before getting out of the stolen car. "He wanted me to tell you that the mission went sideways. He has material for Blaze, but tangos are all around. Need nonsuspect rendezvous point."

That was it. Word for word. Her relief was palpable.

Would they understand, though? They'd better, since she only half understood what she'd told them herself.

The man with the green eyes sitting across from her extended a hand. "I'm Zac." He nodded to the man beside her. "This is Finn."

"Nice to meet you." She shook his hand, then Finn's. Even knowing Wyatt the way she did, it still came as a surprise when their hands engulfed hers. There weren't many people who could make her feel small.

"Is Wyatt okay?" Finn asked in a low voice.

"He's bruised up. His car got run off the road. Plus this guy named Lexington drugged him a couple of nights ago and chased us through the wilderness yesterday. But Wyatt's mostly fine."

Better than fine, in fact. Her cheeks reddened when she remembered how fine he'd been when she'd been on top of him last night.

"I'm Nadine MacFarlane." The men glanced at each other, then nodded slowly. "I met Wyatt a couple years ago when Linear Tactical set up security for my friend Chloe Westman. He and I reconnected this week."

Reconnected. Canoodled. Had steaming hot sex in a cave. Whatever.

"We've been wondering what the hell was going on," Finn muttered. "We knew there was a problem a few days ago when Wyatt didn't return and we couldn't get in touch with him. Since then, I've spotted four different vehicles parked in town today. All too close to Linear employees' houses."

She nodded. "Wyatt saw two cars near Kendrick's house. He thinks the people trying to get the computer drive are watching all of you, waiting for him to show up."

Zac nodded. "There was another car near the main turn-off of the Linear property. And Aiden said he got some hinky feeling about a guy who came in asking about classes a few hours ago."

"I trust Aiden's gut about these things," Finn said, meeting Zac's eyes. The two of them were obviously doing some sort of Special Forces nonverbal communication voodoo.

Zac scowled. "I'll notify everyone to watch their backs."

A moment later, both of them tensed and sat up a little straighter, eyes moving to the door.

Instinct told Nadine not to turn her head to see what all the concern was about. She settled for looking out of the corner of her eye. There was a man standing near the door who'd just come in. He was big like Zac and Finn, but that was the only thing that made him stand out.

"What's wrong?" she whispered.

"That's probably a tango," Finn explained. "One of the guys from the cars we've been talking about."

He looked like an ordinary person to her untrained eye. "How can you tell?"

"For one thing," Zac murmured, "this is a small town. We know everybody, and he's new. On top of that, there's a bulge under his shirt. That's a weapon. Not exactly uncommon here in Wyoming, but it's worth taking note of."

Wow. They had noticed that about him within seconds. It spoke to their training, for sure. Wyatt was the same way. He could spot things like that in the blink of an eye, then make adjustments to his actions based on that intel.

Her phone buzzed with another text.

Tell Z & F unsub just walked in. He's carrying.

She had to stifle a laugh.

"What?" Finn asked.

She turned to show them Wyatt's text. Both men shook their heads.

"Tell Wyatt this isn't my first day at school." Zac rolled his eyes. "And not to make me have to come kick his ass."

They spotted him already. Everything's okay.

Close enough.

"Wyatt is an overprotective hen," Finn muttered.

Zac raised a dark eyebrow. "Sounds like someone else I know."

Finn rolled his eyes. "Pretty sure you're just as protective about your wife as I am about Charlie."

Zac kept an eye on the man as he leaned toward her. "Tell Wyatt to meet us at Ghost's place tonight around nine p.m. He knows where it is. Get rid of anybody following. We'll make sure Kendrick is there."

"Okay, I'll tell him." She didn't understand all the details about what they were saying, but Wyatt would. These men were a team. She should've known Wyatt wouldn't associate with anybody but the best.

"You head out now and get to Scout. We'll keep that guy here." Finn looked past her to the man in question, who was still waiting for a table but also studying them.

He was there for her, or at least was tailing her to find out who she was. Maybe he'd seen her when they'd driven past Kendrick's house. Maybe they'd been following Zac or Finn.

Or maybe this was all paranoia, and she was reading into innocent actions because she expected trouble. But if she was paranoid, then these trained soldiers were too. That made her feel better.

She slid off the bench and stood. Zac stood and before

she turned away from the table, he murmured in her ear, "You're as lovely and brave as Wyatt said you were. Sorry it's under these circumstances, but we're very happy to finally meet you."

She could feel herself gape as she stared at him. "Wyatt talked about me?" she whispered.

Zac winked. "Hasn't shut up about you for damn near *years*. Thank you for helping him now."

She wanted to ask more, but Finn had already headed for the door, arms outstretched. "Tommy! It's so good to see you, man!" He took the stranger by the shoulder and shuffled him away from the door before the man—who looked surprised and confused—knew what was happening.

As she hurried out the door with her head down, Finn continued the ruse. "Zac! Come meet Tommy. We went to college together."

"Uh, I think you've got the wrong person . . ."

Zac and Finn kept the man pinned with friendliness while Nadine made her escape. His protests faded to nothing as she hurried back to the car.

She liked Wyatt's friends and could see why he called them his brothers.

She rushed to the car. "Everything's okay," she announced before glancing over her shoulder.

The back seat was empty.

Her heart leapt into her throat, threatening to choke her. Had they taken Wyatt? Gotten to him while she was inside?

Should she run back to the diner to tell Zac and Finn? Would that put her in the path of the guy with the gun? What was the right move here?

The passenger door opened, making her jump. "It's me." Wyatt ducked low into the car. "Sorry for scaring you."

"Half to death," she gasped. "Where did you go? I thought somebody took you."

He reached over and grabbed her hand. "I had to make sure you were okay. I couldn't stay here. I had to be somewhere I could get to you easily if you needed me."

She sucked in another deep breath, her heart returning to a normal rhythm. "Finn says you're an overprotective hen. I think I have to agree with him. You shouldn't put yourself in danger to check on me. It's a risk."

"You're worth every risk, spitfire. Might as well accept that now and save us a bunch of arguments."

What exactly was she supposed to say to that? *Hey, don't be so protective of me? Don't make me feel so cared for?*

"But your safety is important too." She squeezed his hand. "So, don't forget that."

He grinned. "Yes, ma'am."

"We're supposed to meet the guys at Ghost's place at nine o'clock tonight. I hope you know what that means."

"Yes. That's a good choice. Gives us a few hours to kill. How do you feel about driving to the next town over and getting a hotel? Resting and showering."

Given how her body ached—all sorts of muscles she hadn't used in a long time—that sounded like heaven.

"There would be nothing I'd like more than . . ." Her words trailed off as she spotted someone past his shoulder, a face she'd never expected to see here.

"What's wrong?" he asked. "Do you see trouble?"

"I-I see . . . No, that can't be right." She shook her head.

Wyatt looked in the direction she was staring. "Yeah. Lexi. Everything has been so crazy there hasn't been a chance for me to mention her yet."

Lexi. Right. Alexandra Adam's nickname for herself. "That's really her? I wasn't sure. She looks a little different than when I last saw her. And I can hardly believe Alexandra is visiting any town in Wyoming, much less one the size of Oak Creek."

After all, she'd been a huge celebrity, the starring actress on one of television's hottest shows . . . *Day's End*. Chloe had worked with her on a daily basis.

Before Alexandra had been arrested for obstruction of justice and filing a false police report. She'd trashed her own studio trailer and left false death threats for herself.

And because of Alexandra's deliberately selfish actions, the studio's security team had been reassigned to watch her and the real stalker had come after Nadine and Chloe. Nadine had nearly burned to death when he'd left her unconscious in a burning building.

Wyatt let out a little sigh. "She's not visiting. She lives here. And she looks a little different because her nose and cheek were broken in prison."

Nadine wasn't sure how she was supposed to feel about that. Her nose had been broken too, when she'd been kicked in the face by a killer.

She wasn't happy at the thought of Alexandra being brutalized in prison. But she wasn't sad that the other woman had gone to prison in the first place. Alexandra had been selfish and manipulative and Nadine and Chloe had paid the price for it.

Nadine let out a soft sigh. "I haven't really kept up with what happened to Alexandra after she went to jail. I had my own trauma to deal with. I'm not sure how I feel about her."

"It's okay to hate her."

Nadine was silent for a long moment. "I don't hate her. She was selfish and generally not a very likable person, but I never hated her. She wasn't the one who tried to kill me."

"That's big of you. Others wouldn't be that forgiving."

She shrugged. "I wasn't unhappy when I heard she was sentenced to actual prison time instead of community service or something. Why is she here in Oak Creek?"

"That's a long story. But basically she had a real stalker

this time—wasn't crying wolf—and ended up here, hiding. One of the LT guys, Gavin Zimmerman, helped her out and they're engaged. She runs one of the town's bars."

"Wow."

"I've been out of town for work most of the time since she arrived. I'm not trying to make any excuses for her, but evidently her life was pretty shitty even when she was a famous movie star. Being used and hurt by people she should've been able to trust."

That was a situation Nadine understood intimately. "Yeah."

"Still doesn't mean you have to forgive her or ever talk to her again. Trust me, I would understand."

"Thank you." She appreciated his understanding, and the fact that he was so solidly on her side.

Alexandra was part of the past she'd been hiding from. Not because Nadine was afraid of the other woman, but because it had been one more thing that was easier to turn her back on than to face.

But that was the coward's way. Maybe it was time to stop being a coward.

Chapter 14

Seeing Alexandra now made Nadine realize she truly didn't hate the other woman. Didn't blame her for what had happened. Nadine wasn't going to jump out and give Alexandra a big hug, but she didn't need to be nervous about seeing Alexandra again.

If the past forty-eight hours had taught Nadine anything, it was that you weren't guaranteed tomorrow to face whatever trauma you were hiding from.

Or maybe it was that trauma found you no matter where you hid.

Either way, she'd learned that she was a damned sight stronger than she'd given herself credit for. If anyone had asked her before yesterday if she'd be able to make it through a situation like she had, she would've scoffed.

But also, God, it was so much to process. Day after day, year after year of nothing and then . . . *everything* all at once.

She was quiet as Wyatt directed them back out of town so they could get to a hotel. A shower sounded heavenly. They drove in different directions to make sure no one was following them, then finally ended up at a hotel about thirty minutes outside of Oak Creek. They grabbed some food to go at the restaurant next door, then barricaded themselves in the room.

As good as it felt to be indoors, fed, and feeling safe, Nadine was still quiet. Wyatt didn't push her to talk—seemed to understand her need to filter through stuff. When she got up to take a shower, he kissed her on the forehead and let her go.

She was both relieved and disappointed to be in the shower alone. She got out, wrapped herself in a towel, and sat on the bed so Wyatt could use it. He still didn't try to force her to talk, merely kissed her on the forehead again. It made her feel cherished.

Wrapped in the towel, she tucked herself up against the headboard of the bed, her mind full of *everything* that had happened—from finding out the truth about Wyatt all the way through to seeing Alexandra today in Oak Creek. She wasn't sure how to process it all, but she couldn't go back to the Nadine she'd been at the beginning of this week.

She didn't realize she was tracing her fingers up and down her burn scars on her legs—that disgusting habit—until she felt Wyatt's fingers tracing along with hers.

She jerked her hand away and looked up at him, horrified. "I'm sorry. That's so gross. I don't know why I do it."

His brown eyes narrowed. "Do what?"

"Trace my scars when I'm not paying attention. My fingers kind of find them and move along the pattern. I'm not doing it on purpose." God, he had to think she was some kind of freak.

"Why would you think that's gross?"

"Because what kind of person traces her own disfigurement? My legs have literally frightened small children."

He studied her legs. She swallowed rapidly, breath uneven as she realized he'd never seen her legs. In their little cave, it had been too dark and then she'd re-dressed before the sun came up.

She tried to scoot away on the bed. "Oh God, let me put my pants back on or at least cover up."

He grabbed her hand to stop her movements, then brought her palm up to his lips. "No, you shouldn't cover up. You don't have to hide. Not from me. Not from anybody."

She looked down at her legs sprawled in front of her. "But the scars are hideous."

He kept his eyes on hers as his fingers traced the same pattern hers had been tracing. "Your scars are proof of your strength. Proof of everything you've lived through. That makes them beautiful."

She looked away. "You're just saying that."

"I'm not. I wouldn't lie to you."

He took her fingers and trailed them along her scars again. She wanted to jerk her hand free. "It's disgusting for me to do that."

"There's nothing wrong with touching irregularities in your skin. It's a habit that soothes the mind, like wrapping a strand of hair around your finger or biting your nails."

"I guess."

He brought his own fingers to stroke down her legs on the largest scars above her knees. "And like it or not, these burns represent a day that changed your life. Everything you've done or thought since then has been filtered through the lens of those hours." He leaned down until his lips hovered over her legs. "I look at them and see strength. Fortitude. The same thing I saw while you ran through the woods last night."

She ran her fingers through the back of his thick hair as he kissed her legs. "Thank you."

"Plus the best of us have scars." He sat up and pointed to

a puffy scar on his right shoulder. "I earned this one in a gunfight with a kidnapper."

Next, he pointed to his left ribs. "Under all this bruising is a long, thin scar from a knife. Collapsed my lung. That was a close call."

He tapped his left shoulder blade. "And the burn marks you saw are from when I was in that cell. I can't see them, but I'm very aware that they're there by the lack of elasticity in that part of my skin. I remember how much it hurt. I can't begin to imagine what you went through."

She shrugged. "I was unconscious for most of it."

"We both know the initial pain of a burn is just the beginning."

She met his eyes. He understood. Unless someone had lived through a traumatic burn themselves, they truly couldn't understand, as much as they might want to.

"Sometimes, I still . . ." She closed her eyes, pressing a fist against her lips.

He brought her hand back down. "Tell me, beautiful. Remember? Don't turn your back on the enemy, even when the enemy is your past."

She wrapped her arms around herself and looked into his brown eyes. He was lending her his strength again.

"Sometimes, I still wake up screaming. Trapped in that burning building. There was so much smoke, and I was in so much pain." The burns. The broken bones. "And I wasn't sure I was going in the right direction. I can actually taste the terror of knowing I might not make it out."

"Nadine—"

Her hands fell helplessly to her sides. "I should be over this by now! I got hurt, yes. But Chloe *died*. She literally died and she's already over it. But not me, I'm still hiding in the middle of fucking Idaho over two years later!"

She stopped, unable to believe she'd said those words—used that language—out loud. "I'm sorry."

He gripped her shoulders. "Oh hell no, don't you be sorry. Maybe it's time to get a little pissed. Mad at Travis, mad at Lexi, mad at the universe, mad that what happened has stolen so much of your life."

Her hands balled into fists. She *was* mad. "I'm sick and tired of being afraid. And I'm as pissed at myself as I am anybody or anything else."

He pulled her into his arms, and she gripped his naked back, digging in with her nails. "You are the only one who can't see how strong you are. Some people would've been terrified to ever be alone again after what had happened to you, but you haven't flinched from it. You have nightmares, but you keep going. It's all a part of the healing process."

"I've hidden myself away. Haven't been on a date in over two years."

He leaned back so they could be eye to eye. "Neither have I. Maybe we were waiting for the right time to be with each other."

She trailed nails up his back until they dug into his scalp. "I don't want to wait anymore. Turn out the lights and let's continue healing."

"How about I leave the lights on and we continue healing? I want to see you. Feel you. Taste you."

She couldn't help herself. "But my scars . . ."

"You should never be ashamed. Your scars are a badge of honor. Scars mean you know how to survive."

WYATT HOPED some of what he was saying was getting through to her because it was the God's honest truth. He loved every bit of her body, including the scars.

Especially the scars.

She yanked his head toward her and kissed him. He could taste the aggression in it, the frustration, but he didn't mind. Whatever demons she was fighting, he was willing to offer his body to take the abuse.

She wanted to feel in control? He could help her do that. Wanted to feel strong? She already was. He would merely enable her to see it.

He pulled at the towel wrapped around her torso, letting it fall to the bed around her, then began kissing his way down her body. He wasn't in a rush this time—there were no murderers searching for them, no wilderness, no storms. Just them.

He paid special attention to both those beautiful, lush breasts until she moaned and squirmed under him. Then continued down her belly, across her hips, and down to her legs.

He kissed the scars.

He kissed them because he wanted her to know he would never find them anything but beautiful. But he didn't stay focused on them for long because he knew the scarred skin wouldn't have the same pleasure receptors as the rest of her.

But mostly because although the scars were a part of her, they were only a part. He wanted the *whole*.

Slowly, he worked his way back up her inner thighs. The scars trailed off to smoother skin, and he slid her legs open and kissed to where he really wanted to be.

He teased her. With his mouth, with his fingers . . . in all the ways he'd dreamed of teasing her. He nipped and sucked and licked until she alternated between moans and gasps, fingers clutching his hair.

It was only after her back arched up off the bed and she ground herself against his mouth while calling his name, then collapsed, limp, that he stopped.

But he wasn't done.

He grabbed one of the condoms he'd bought when they'd stopped earlier and eased it on.

His gaze slid up her body to rest on her face and his heart skipped a beat at the look of utter trust and contentment in those hazel eyes.

"You're so unbelievably beautiful. Inside and out."

She held out her arms to him and he went, moving between her legs and easing himself slowly inside her. His eyes stayed focused on hers as he moved, driving them slowly, gently back up to the pinnacle.

His eyes were still on hers, the only place he wanted to be, as they fell.

Chapter 15

They spent every moment in each other's arms until it was time to leave for the rendezvous. After their second bout of lovemaking, Nadine fell asleep. Wyatt hated to wake her as the sun went down, but he wanted to leave plenty of time to get to Dorian and Ray's cabin at the correct time.

That place wasn't the easiest to find. Smack dab in the middle of the Wyoming wilderness about ten miles outside of Oak Creek. No real roads led to it; you could only get so far before having to walk the last quarter mile. The cabin itself wasn't on any map, nor did it run on public electricity or water.

Dorian and Ray Lindstrom had better reasons than anybody for living off the grid, especially since Ray—a.k.a. Grace Brandt—was officially a dead domestic terrorist according to all government records.

Until recently, they had lived farther out in the wilderness, far away from anyone, including their Linear Tactical family. They'd needed time to heal after what had happened to them.

The fact that Ray and Dorian had moved so much closer

to Oak Creek spoke volumes about how much their lives had changed since they had reunited.

How two jagged, broken people could heal each other.

Knowing the location of this cabin was still top secret. Only those Dorian trusted with his life, with *Ray's* life, knew about it. So Wyatt had been very careful to make sure no one followed them as they made their way deeper into the forest. After parking next to Zac's and Finn's vehicles, he took Nadine's hand to walk to the cabin.

Dorian and Ray's place blended into the wooded environment so well, it was almost unrecognizable from the outside—especially in the dark. It was also built partially underground, hiding a great deal of its size. Wyatt wasn't at all surprised when Dorian met them at the door, aware of their arrival.

"Hey, Ghost." Wyatt used the big man's code name as he walked up and shook his hand while slapping him on the shoulder. "Thanks for lending us your place. This is my friend Nadine MacFarlane. Nadine, Dorian Lindstrom, one of my Special Forces brothers."

Dorian smiled and grabbed Nadine's hand in his. "Can't tell you how good it is to meet you in person, although I'm sorry it's under these circumstances. This guy has been mildly obsessed with you since he met you."

Wyatt was glad when Nadine smiled. "He's accused himself of being my stalker."

"At least he's one with your best interests at heart."

They moved inside the cabin, and Dorian introduced Nadine to Ray. As always, Dorian's petite wife was a little standoffish, but not unfriendly.

Zac and Finn were outside keeping watch. Kendrick showed up a few minutes later with his laptop.

"Seriously, Dorian, is it too much to ask for you to get a house where there are street signs?" Kendrick shook his head as he began setting up his computer at the kitchen table. "Maybe it is. Then how about actual *streets*?"

Dorian grinned. "You're mad because your specialized GPS couldn't find our place. What's the point in being off the grid if you're not *off the grid*?"

Wyatt sat back on the couch, watching the show with his hand resting loosely on Nadine's thigh.

Kendrick clicked away on his laptop for a few seconds. "Is this the Lexington who's been chasing you? Zac and Finn mentioned him." He spun the screen to show Wyatt and Nadine a picture.

"Yep." That was definitely the fucker who'd beat the shit out of him when he was drugged. Wyatt was determined this guy would not get his hands on Nadine.

"Meet George Lexington. I found lots of fun info about him."

"He's the human trafficker?" Nadine asked.

Kendrick shook his head. "Oh hell no. This guy couldn't organize a Girl Scout meeting—"

"Whoa now." Wyatt held up a hand. "Girl Scout meetings take more organization than most people realize."

"—much less a human trafficking network," Kendrick continued without stopping. "He's a heavy. A thug for hire."

Wyatt nodded. "All right, so he's no Einstein. That's good."

"But he's definitely brutal. He's left a blood trail a mile long. Guy is sadistic as fuck."

Wyatt shot Kendrick a look when Nadine stiffened beside him.

"Sorry." Kendrick gave her an apologetic smile. "What I meant is, Lexington's not someone any of us want to be friends with. He mostly works around Vegas and Reno, but evidently, he felt it was worth his time for an interstate pursuit. He's been after the drive—and you—because someone offered him an insane amount of money to get it."

"Who?" Nadine asked.

Kendrick winked at her. "Imma find that out for you right now." He held up his hand. "Drive?"

Wyatt handed the small electronic box to him. Kendrick studied the drive, turning on its power switch, then connecting it to his computer.

Nadine sat quietly beside him on the couch as Kendrick worked. Even after resting some today—when he could keep his hands off her—they were both exhausted. But it was mostly over. Now that he had backup and Lexington's ID, Wyatt was going to make sure the threat was eliminated.

"You okay?" he whispered to her.

"Yeah. I'm hoping Kendrick can get the info off the drive and everything won't be in vain. If what we did saves lives, then it all will have been worth it."

She was going to have a hard, emotional crash after this. Dealing with the loss of her home, her possessions, the exhaustion, and the aches from what her body had been through was going to hit all at once.

But he was going to be right there with her. He squeezed her leg, wishing he could whisk her away.

"All right, you don't want to play nice, that's fine." Everyone ignored Kendrick since he was talking to his computer. His fingers moved faster on the keyboard than Wyatt could ever dream of typing.

It was like the rest of the world didn't exist for the younger man as he worked, alternating between muttered curses and delighted laughter.

Kendrick had been at it for nearly an hour. Wyatt and Nadine were both resting on the couch with their eyes closed when Dorian tapped Wyatt on the shoulder.

"You got anyone outside I should know about besides Zac and Finn?"

"No, they were going to remain about two hundred yards out." Wyatt gave a tiny nod to Ray. "They figured it was crowded enough with the three of us, but they'd be around if we needed them."

There was more than enough room in the cabin for five people, but given her past, Ray didn't like to be around anyone but Dorian for extended periods of time. The guys knew it and respected it. Wyatt would've stayed outside if it weren't for wanting to give Nadine a safe place to rest while Kendrick worked.

"Then we've got problems."

Nadine's eyes popped open. "What problems?"

"Somebody's out there who's not part of our team." Dorian gestured for them to come toward what looked to be a large, plain cabinet—a hutch where you'd keep dishes or something. But when he opened it, there definitely weren't any dishes.

It was a damn command center with multiple screens showing a huge radius around the house. Infrared surveillance, heat signatures, markers with all sorts of triggers that would let them know when someone was nearby.

Wyatt had been on military missions that didn't provide as much detail about the area being infiltrated as this did.

"I thought you guys were off the grid," Nadine whispered.

Ray shrugged, taking her place next to Dorian. "We're off the government's grid. We built our own."

Dorian pointed at two blinking dots. "That's Zac and Finn. But someone else tripped our outer perimeter." He pointed to the other end of the screen where dots had appeared.

Ray placed her hand on Dorian's. "You don't think

it's . . ." she trailed off, silently communicating with her husband, who obviously knew what she was trying to say.

"No. Too much is different. Wrong direction, wrong time of day. It's not them."

Ray nodded but didn't say anything further.

"Something I should know?" Wyatt asked. "You been having problems with strangers in the woods?"

He wasn't too concerned about it. The Lindstroms were more than capable of eliminating any threat to their safety.

"Not a problem exactly," Dorian gingerly ran his fingers along the screen, "but definitely an anomaly."

"Dorian, we have to be sure," Ray said softly.

Nadine looked to Wyatt in confusion, but he didn't know what to tell her. He had no idea what his friends were talking about either. Their secrets weren't important because Wyatt trusted them, and that was all that mattered.

Dorian slipped an arm around his wife. "We will be. We'll take tranqs as primary."

"Ghost, talk to me," Wyatt said. "What the hell is going on?"

"Are you sure you weren't followed? Phone wasn't traced?"

Wyatt nodded. "One hundred percent. Dumped my phone days ago, and there is no way anyone followed us here."

They'd driven for more than an hour to make sure of it.

"They found us through the drive," Kendrick said.

"What?" Wyatt turned to look at him. "Is that possible?"

Kendrick ran a hand over his short, cropped hair. "That's why it has its own power source. When it turns on, it lets out an electronic ping. If someone like our buddy Lexington knows to look for the ping, it's like a homing beacon."

Shit. Wyatt turned to Nadine. "That's how they found us at your house. I thought maybe they had run some sort of facial recognition software on you from the hotel, but it's because I turned the drive on to make sure it was still intact."

He turned back to Ray and Dorian. "But you think it could be somebody else out there? Not our tangos?"

Dorian shook his head. "No, I think it's your bad guys. However, we need to be aware that there is the possibility of . . . *neutrals* out in these woods. Like I said, they've never moved at night or from that direction, but we all need to make sure we're not trigger happy, just in case."

The look Dorian gave him promised he'd explain more later. When it came to things out in the wilderness, Wyatt trusted Dorian's instincts more than anyone on the planet— and trusted his friend's judgment just as much.

"Roger that. Tranqs it is. I'll make sure Zac and Finn know."

And he would make sure Dorian explained exactly what was going on later. Dorian and Ray had been through enough. The team wouldn't let them go through whatever problems they were facing alone, even if that was their preference.

"Shit."

Everyone turned toward Kendrick to find him standing as he did something nobody at Linear had ever seen him do. He deliberately shut his computer down.

"We've got bigger problems than Lexington or whoever is after you in the woods right now."

"That can't be good," Nadine whispered.

Kendrick scrubbed a hand down his face. "I know who's paying Lexington to get the drive back."

Wyatt grabbed Nadine's hand. "Who?"

"Mosaic."

Wyatt and Dorian both cursed.

Kendrick nodded. "This drive is a much bigger deal than you thought. From what I could see before I was booted out completely, it contains details of the inner workings of Mosaic. Evidently, they've branched out from treason and cyber terror to actual human trafficking."

"I don't understand." Nadine whispered. "What is Mosaic? I've never heard of them."

Wyatt squeezed her hand. "It's a criminal organization. A pretty name for a very ugly group of people. They're highly organized, but the leadership is almost completely hidden. They're bad news on all possible fronts."

"You need to get this info to Ian DeRose," Dorian said to Kendrick. "If it's Mosaic, he's going to want to know."

Kendrick nodded. "He'll be my first call. Ian and the Zodiac team are the only ones who'll be equipped to move on the info."

"Kendrick," Ray said, her eyes narrowed, "do we have Mosaic soldiers outside our door right now?"

"How many people did you detect through your surveillance system?" Kendrick began to disconnect the rest of his equipment.

"Half dozen at most," Dorian said.

"Then it's not Mosaic. If it were Mosaic, there would be a hell of a lot more. It's probably Lexington following the last pings." Kendrick wrapped a cord around his hand. "I hid you as best I could—made it seem like the ping was a malfunction, bouncing all over the place. Once you take care of whoever's out there, your house should be secure again, Ghost."

Kendrick looked back and forth between Wyatt and Dorian. "What's on this drive is time-sensitive. Once Mosaic finds out someone could potentially access their internal info, they'll come at it no-holds-barred. I need to get it out of here and to someone who can help me. This isn't something I can handle on my own."

"You're going to bring Neo in on this?" Dorian asked.

"She's my best option. Maybe my only option."

"Fine," Dorian said. "I'm calling Zac so he can get you to safety."

Kendrick rolled his eyes. "I don't need a babysitter."

Dorian dropped a hand on the man's shoulder. "I know, Blaze. But that drive is too important—*you're* too important —to take a chance with. There's been bad guys crawling around Oak Creek all day. We'd send backup no matter who it was."

Kendrick reluctantly nodded, and Dorian was on the phone with Zac a few seconds later.

Kendrick turned to Wyatt. "This is going to leave you shorthanded against Lexington and his buddies."

He slipped an arm around Nadine and gave the other man a smile. "Their five to our five? I'll take those odds any day."

But he'd give anything to make it Lexington's five to their *four*, wishing Nadine were anywhere but here. Especially with how worried she looked as she watched Kendrick finish packing up.

"Hey." He turned her so they were face-to-face. "Lexington and his men don't know we know they're out there. And if you thought I was great with SERE training, wait until you see Dorian. His code name is Ghost because he can move in and out of places without anyone ever seeing."

"Okay."

"We're going to take them down without them knowing what hit them. That's what we were trained to do."

Chapter 16

This was happening. Everyone was moving around Nadine, and she wasn't quite sure what to do with herself.

The possibility of a deadly showdown had been there ever since the first bottle bomb had flown through her kitchen window. Maybe since the moment Wyatt first showed up at the Fresh Market. But the sight of an entire room full of weapons solidified that it was really happening.

She had thought the cabinet holding the surveillance screens was impressive, but then Kendrick had left with Zac, and Ray had flipped a switch on the back wall . . .

The whole wall moved.

The whole damn wall moved to reveal some sort of secret compartment straight out of a *Terminator* movie. Guns of all kinds, knives of all sizes, and . . . crossbows. At least four of them.

Nadine turned to stare at Wyatt, then Dorian and Ray. Who owned such an arsenal?

Wyatt had told her the couple had their reasons for being off the grid. She would trust that they had their reasons for being equipped heavily enough to take down a small army.

It would all certainly come in handy now.

Dorian handed a pair of guns to Wyatt, who checked them with practiced efficiency.

Ray accepted a gun and a small crossbow. Her fingers caressed the weapon with a gentle—almost lover-like—touch. She was obviously familiar with the weapons in her hands.

Ray was petite, nearly fragile looking. The type of woman Nadine was normally afraid of accidentally stepping on and squashing or something. Nadine towered over her by probably eight inches and had at least eighty pounds on her.

But there was nothing remotely damsel in distress about Ray. She was coolly efficient and confident while she prepared for this situation. Ray was a trained soldier, like the men in the room.

Dorian looked over his shoulder at her. "Nadine, do you know how to handle a weapon?"

"Uh, not a crossbow, but I can fire a handgun."

Wyatt winked at her and walked to her with a gun Dorian had handed him.

"This is a SIG Sauer P320." He pressed the gun into her hand. "Here's the safety lever. You click that off, point, and pull the trigger. Easy breezy."

Her laugh was tinged with hysteria. "Yeah. *Easy breezy.*"

Wyatt stroked a thumb down her cheek. "Well, easy breezy compared to a crossbow."

"Right." She forced another smile. "We'll start training on that tomorrow."

He kissed her forehead. "You're the most amazing woman I've ever known."

"Yeah? I'm pretty sure Ray could kick my ass." She leaned her head down against his chest.

He let out a short bark of laughter. "Ray could kick all of

our asses. You're still the most amazing woman I've ever known."

"You be safe out there." God, she couldn't stand the thought of Lexington getting his hands on Wyatt. She looked down at the holster he'd slipped on over his broad shoulders. "Two guns, huh? Pretty tough stuff."

He held up the one in his hand. "This is a tranquilizer. The others hold real bullets. I believe in keeping myself covered. Whatever we find out there, we'll handle it."

One of the displays on the living room wall pinged. Dorian's jaw tightened before he moved past them to check the alarm. "They're within half a mile now."

Wyatt looked down at his phone. "Zac messaged me. He and Kendrick are out safe. He'll get Blaze where he needs to go to work on the drive."

There was hardly the time to feel relieved before a second alarm went off. This one was louder, more assertive.

Ray reached for a tablet. "The inner perimeter's been breached. They're splitting up." She tapped the screen a few times before it revealed five men approaching the cabin.

Nadine's heart beat triple time, and her stomach tightened painfully. It was hard to hear anything over the rush of blood in her ears. How could the three of them be so businesslike about an ambush?

Yet that was exactly how they acted as they slipped in earpieces for communication. "You ready?" Dorian asked Wyatt, who nodded.

Wyatt slipped an arm around her waist and pulled her in for a hard kiss. "I'll be right back. Stay with Ray."

With a wink, he was gone.

WYATT AND DORIAN had been in a number of skirmishes

like this in their Special Forces years. Finn had been right there with them.

This wasn't the first time they'd faced a relatively unknown foe in the dark. But it was the first time his enemies were coming with the intent to harm someone Wyatt wasn't sure he could live without.

"I've got two unsubs in my sights." Finn's voice came through clearly in the communication devices in their ears.

"Roger that," Dorian responded. "They don't know we know they're out here. Our best bet is to let them come toward the house, and we'll take them out from behind."

"Agreed," Finn said.

Wyatt agreed that was the best tactical plan, but he didn't like it. Didn't like letting the bad guys get close to the house —close to Nadine—even when he could see that it gave his team the logistic advantage.

"We can't let them get inside the cabin." Wyatt moved behind some of the bigger trees toward the north.

"Agreed," Dorian said. "Finn, I'm going to bring you tranquilizers. Let's only use lethal force if we have to."

"Roger that. I'm on my way to that boulder southwest of your house for pickup. But we do know that they are not going to afford us the same courtesy, right? They'll be shooting to kill."

Wyatt could tell Finn was on the move though his breathing stayed even as he ran.

"It's unlikely, but we could possibly have innocents in the vicinity." Dorian said. "So, just in case, tranqs."

"Dorian, you do know using tranquilizers means these guys will be able to locate your cabin," Wyatt pointed out. "They may not know who you are, but they will know of this place's existence."

Dorian had worked pretty fucking hard to keep the existence of his home a well-guarded secret.

"I know. But tranqs anyway."

"Roger that." Wyatt and Finn both said it at the same time. There was damned near nothing as important to Dorian as his and Ray's privacy. If he was willing to risk it, then there was something important going on.

Finn knew it too. "You're going to have to give us the lowdown soon, Ghost. Time to get the gossip mill running."

Dorian's voice was low. "Let's eliminate these bastards first."

They agreed on which direction they'd each move in from and silently began to do what Uncle Sam had taught them to do: find the threat and eliminate it.

Dorian had been right; the bad guys were expecting them to be inside the house, leaving their six almost completely unguarded. It took only a few minutes for four of the men to be shot with the tranquilizers and fall uncon-scious. Finn and Wyatt took out one each, while Dorian found and eliminated two.

They circled, looking for the one they hadn't gotten yet.

"I've got eyes on the last guy." Finn's quiet voice came through a few minutes later. "He's coming around wide, west of the house. I'll circle back and take him."

"Roger that," Dorian responded. "I'll let Ray know everything's almost handled and we'll be in soon."

Good. The sooner Wyatt had his own eyes back on Nadine and knew she was safe, the better he would feel. He was already heading back toward the house, expecting an update at any moment from Finn, when he heard a shout from the north side of the cabin.

"No! Why—"

The speaker fell silent. Wyatt ran toward the sound, making sure to keep under the cover of the trees in case this was an ambush. When he arrived at the place where the sound had come from, he found Finn crouched over one of the unsubs, who was lying on the ground.

"Is that the fifth guy?"

Wyatt could barely make out Finn in the darkness. He was checking the man's pulse. "Yeah. He doubled back and circled around the other way. He's dead. Shot."

"You?"

"Wasn't me. I heard him yell and took off running this direction."

Wyatt touched the monitor in his ear. "Dorian, did you kill somebody and fail to mention it?" He almost hoped Dorian would say yes. That would at least explain what was going on.

"Not me."

What the actual fuck then?

"Dorian, we've got a dead guy here. Could these be the people you were alluding to earlier helping us out?" Finn was obviously just as confused as Wyatt.

"Negative." Dorian's voice was beyond sure. "Those people are not in play."

"Could it be Ray?" Wyatt asked. They were running out of options. She was every bit as trained as they were. "Would she have come out here without notifying you?"

God, he hoped she hadn't left Nadine alone inside the house.

"Is your dead guy shot with a crossbow?" Dorian asked.

"Negative," Finn responded. "Gunshots to the head. Close range with a silencer."

"Then it wasn't Ray."

Finn and Wyatt nodded at each other. Ray's use of a crossbow was legendary—if she was going to take someone out, that would be her weapon of choice.

"Who did this, then?" Wyatt couldn't wrap his brain around it. Finn stood up, shaking his head.

"We've got another problem," Dorian said less than a minute later. "More specifically, another bad guy dead. One of the men I tranqed has now been assassinated."

"What the fuck?" Finn muttered.

Wyatt couldn't agree more. "Everybody check the guys you left unconscious. We need to figure out what the hell is happening."

He and Finn both took off in different directions, neither of them moving at full speed. They wanted to be able to keep an eye out for whoever this vigilante was. It didn't make any sense.

"You guys, whoever is doing this isn't a friendly," Wyatt whispered into the comm unit. "None of our people would kill an unconscious man."

"Agreed," Dorian said. "I'm letting Ray know something's not right."

A few minutes later, Finn came on the comm unit with a curse. "The first guy I tranqed is dead also. Head shot."

"Shit. Watch your six," Wyatt muttered. Something about this stank to high heaven.

"Yeah. Back at you."

Keeping a lookout all around him, Wyatt found the tango he'd taken down. He cursed as he got close enough to see that this guy had met the same fate as his friends.

But the noise of the forest had already picked back up around the dead guy—which meant this hadn't happened in the past couple of minutes. He might have been killed right after Wyatt rendered him unconscious. Definitely dead before the man who yelled had been shot.

Why had that guy yelled at all? And why had he been asking *why* with his final words unless he'd recognized the person who'd come to kill him?

"My first guy is dead too," Dorian reported. "Been that way for a while."

"Someone is killing his own men," Wyatt muttered into the comm unit. "Must have come in after the main group."

"Why would someone do that?" Finn asked. "Doesn't make any sense."

"I think he killed all the unconscious guys first, then went back for the final guy who was closest to the house."

"But why?" Dorian asked. "It weakens them."

Oh shit. Wyatt began sprinting back to the cabin, now not wasting any time worrying about a trap.

"It was a ruse to keep us out here. He was by the house when he killed the last guy, then we've been running around trying to figure out what's going on. Meanwhile . . ."

Wyatt pushed for every bit of speed he had, terror eating at him.

"The killer's inside the cabin."

Chapter 17

After he winked at her, Nadine watched Wyatt follow Dorian through a door that opened to some stairs and probably led to a secret exit.

She scratched at the ache in her chest. What if she never saw Wyatt again? This wasn't some game. Wyatt might have tranquilizers, but Lexington's men definitely didn't.

"It's okay." Ray placed a gentle hand on Nadine's arm. "They know what they're doing. They're a team."

"I'm surprised you didn't go with them. You don't strike me as someone who chooses to sit out the action. You certainly look comfortable with weapons." She pointed to the crossbow in Ray's hand.

Ray's smile was thin. "I can fight, but I choose not to when possible. That choice was taken from me once."

"Oh. I see." Nadine didn't see at all, but what else was there to say?

"Dorian has spent our relationship trying to give me that opportunity—the choice *not* to fight—and I love him for it." Her eyes narrowed as she studied the screen in front of her.

"But make no mistake, I can fight when I need to. And if an enemy enters this house, they won't leave alive."

Nadine didn't have a drop of doubt that was true.

Not that it calmed her nerves much. Wyatt was out there, outnumbered and in danger.

She paced the small living room with her Sig in hand. She kept looking down to make sure she knew where the safety switch was in case she needed to use it.

Ray was the opposite, waiting still and patient for word, checking the monitors every once in a while. She touched a finger to her earpiece. "Roger."

Nadine wished she had an earpiece. "What?"

"They're outside, met up with Finn. They're sweeping the perimeter."

"That's good, right?"

Ray nodded. "Yes. They both sound focused."

Ray pressed her hand to her ear again a few minutes later. "They're splitting up, about to flank the intruders. Use the element of surprise and come in from behind them."

A few moments of silence passed. Nadine's heart hammered in her chest. She wanted to know what was going on but they couldn't report if they were in the middle of fighting for their lives.

After a few minutes, she was going to crawl out of her own skin. "Are you worried?"

"No. Dorian always comes back to me."

Ray's quiet assurance helped Nadine some, but relief still pooled through her a little while later when Ray put her fingers back up to her earpiece. "Roger that. Good to hear."

Nadine nearly jumped on her. "What happened?"

"They're okay." Ray smiled wide. "It's going well— almost over. They'll be coming back to the house soon."

She leaned heavily against the wall. "Thank God. I guess I didn't expect it to be that simple."

"Sometimes it works out that way. These guys obviously didn't expect the level of security we have here." Ray patted her shoulder. "It's all over. You can breathe."

Nadine did better than breathe. She placed the Sig on the table, thankful she didn't need it, and walked toward the kitchen for a glass of water.

Once she had Wyatt alone, she wasn't going to let him out of her sight until at least next year. What they'd done in the hotel today was nothing compared to what she was going to do to him once she had her hands—and lips—on him with no hurry, no danger, just *them*.

She wanted to show him how beautiful he made her feel. That his words about her scars and her strength were right.

That she was *ready*.

Ready for what, she wasn't exactly sure. But definitely ready to not live in her frightened little bubble anymore.

She filled the glass with water and took a sip. She and Wyatt could figure it out together.

"Finally have you all alone." The voice directly behind her—male and gut-punchingly familiar—hit her awareness at the same time the touch of metal licked the back of her neck.

She would never forget his voice.

"Lexington," she whispered.

"Put your hands behind your back without making a sound," he ordered. "I don't want to kill your friend in the other room, but believe me, I will."

Nadine set the water glass down and put her hands behind her back. Should she yell? He secured her with a zip tie, pulling it tight enough to make her wince.

"Nadine, we've got a problem," Ray called out from the living room. "One of the tangoes is still on the loose. The guys are searching."

Lexington snickered as he grabbed Nadine's arm,

yanking her into place in front of him. Nadine wanted to scream, to warn Ray, but all she could feel was the gun against her temple.

Ray's footsteps grew louder. She was on her way to the kitchen. "Evidently, one of the bad guys killed his own men as a diversion and— Oh, I guess that would be you," she finished as she saw Lexington using Nadine as a human shield.

"Put down the gun," he growled, "or I'll shoot her." He jabbed the gun against Nadine's neck.

Ray bent, one hand in the air, lowering her gun to the floor in front of her.

"Now you're going to talk into that earpiece of yours and tell the guys outside to come in."

Ray raised an eyebrow. "Not going to happen."

"You sure about that?" His fingers tightened around Nadine's bicep until she whimpered, no matter how she fought against reacting. Lexington pressed the gun against her temple. "Do it, now."

"Fine." Ray held her hand up to her ear, but Nadine realized right away it wasn't the same ear she'd been using to communicate with the guys. She was tricking Lexington. "Ghost, Scout. We need some assistance in the kitchen. Thanks."

"Tie your hands." Lexington tossed Ray a zip tie. She secured her wrists in place, teeth gritted the entire time. "Good girl."

"How did you manage to get in here?" Ray asked. She never took her eyes from him.

"Your guys out there aren't the only ones trained in warfare," Lexington explained. "You have to make sacrifices if you want to get ahead."

Ray's eyes narrowed. "Like killing your own men?"

"I did what I had to do."

She let out a sigh. "Believe it or not, I respect that."

Nadine didn't have any doubt Ray was trying to distract him. He was expecting the guys to come any minute and no doubt planned to shoot them.

Ray probably had some sort of plan, but Nadine didn't know what it was. But she wasn't going to sit here and keep being used as a human shield. She'd found out the hard way years ago when she and Chloe had been kidnapped and tied up that her wrist could still be dislocated if she pressed it the right way—a byproduct of a fight with a bully when she was a kid.

Though it hurt like hell, it was convenient when she needed to get out of restraints.

She'd been too late when she'd done it with Chloe. Too weak to make a difference in the situation.

She wasn't going to let that happen this time.

"What do you want with the drive?" Ray asked, continuing the stalling. "Who are you working for?"

"Don't worry about that."

"We could pay you more," she told him. "I have contacts willing to give top dollar. It doesn't have to go down like this."

"Oh, it certainly does," he crooned. His mouth was close to Nadine's ear, making her skin crawl. "I intend to kill that son of a bitch boyfriend of yours, then I'll have a good time with you. Payment for breaking my nose. This is personal."

Nadine focused on her wrist. One . . . two . . . three. Sweat broke out on her brow as she bit her tongue at the agony blistering through her wrist.

Her wrist slid out of the restraints. She kept her hands behind her back.

Ray's eyes narrowed. Did she understand? Did it matter? Ray's hands were restrained—not much help against a gun.

It would be up to Nadine to fight Lexington. But how?

He was so much bigger than her, and she didn't have her pepper spray.

He focused his attention on Ray while he babbled about his Special Forces training. Blatantly bragging, since it was that training that had helped him get past Dorian and Wyatt.

If she could manage a few solid punches, it might buy enough time for Ray to get to the gun on the floor. It was their only chance.

She'd have to do it right the first time, since there wouldn't be a second opportunity. She tried to signal Ray with her eyes, tilting her head, but she had no idea if the other woman understood.

Which was why she used every ounce of her strength in slamming an elbow into Lexington's gut, gritting her teeth at the pain that shot through her injured wrist. At the same time, she stomped on his instep—all moves learned from her classic self-defense training.

But it didn't quite work.

"You bitch!" Lexington didn't drop the gun, and Nadine screamed as he yanked her hair viciously, pulling her head back against him, putting the gun up to her head.

This was it. Nadine squeezed her eyes tight; she couldn't help it.

Then . . . nothing. No gunfire, no pain. Just a big thump on the floor behind her.

Nadine opened her eyes to find Lexington lying on the ground with a knife sticking out of his throat.

Very dead.

"Basic Bad Guy 101." Ray stood over him at Nadine's side, her hands free. "Never have someone tie themselves up, dumbass." She turned to Nadine. "You okay?"

"Yeah. I . . . I—" She couldn't pull any thoughts together. "Thank you."

Ray smiled. "We make a good team."

"Ray! Nadine!" Wyatt and Dorian burst into the house and rushed to the kitchen. They lowered their weapons as they sized up the situation in a few glances.

"Got worried when you didn't respond to our reports," Dorian said.

"Seems like you missed one," Ray said. "We handled it."

Wyatt pulled Nadine against his chest. "You're okay," he whispered. Was he assuring her or himself? It didn't matter.

Dorian put an arm around Ray. "Lexington was a full-on psychopath," he sighed, scrubbing a hand over his cheek as he looked down at the dead man. "When he found out we were only tranquilizing his guys, he killed them all and used our confusion as a distraction to get in here."

Cradling her injured wrist, Nadine pulled back from Wyatt and whispered to Ray, "You saved my life."

Ray shook her head. "No. You saved your own life. I could've killed him at any time, but I couldn't take the risk of him getting a shot off on you first. Getting yourself free gave me the chance I needed."

Pride beamed in Wyatt's eyes, and he bent to kiss the top of her head. But then a curse flew from his lips when he saw her wrist jutting out at an angle that was definitely not natural.

"What the hell happened? Did Lexington do that?"

Why did Wyatt's voice sound so far away? She shook her head to clear the cobwebs.

"No, I dislocated it to get out of the zip tie. I did that when Chloe and I were trapped, but I was too late then, too weak."

Both Dorian and Ray were giving her sympathetic nods, but they seemed to sway on their feet.

"I didn't want to be too weak this time."

"Oh, sweetheart, you weren't." Wyatt was gentler with her now, helping her cradle her wrist while pressing a kiss against her forehead. "You're the most amazing woman I've ever met."

"You said that to me already." His brown eyes were all she could see.

"Then how about . . . you're the most amazing woman I've ever met and I'm in love with you."

She wanted to kiss him, wanted to tell him she felt the same—that the past forty-eight hours had proved it to her. But the darkness that had been squeezing in on her vision for the past few minutes wouldn't let her go. It kept taking up more of her sight.

"Oh no . . ." she whispered.

Then completely passed out.

Chapter 18

Wyatt caught Nadine as she fell and lowered her to the ground, careful not to injure her wrist any further.

"She okay?" Finn asked.

"I think so. Got a little overwhelmed by the whole situation, not to mention dislocating her wrist to do what she could to help."

Her eyes were already starting to flutter. She'd be awake again in a couple minutes, probably embarrassed that her brain had needed to shut down for a second to regroup.

"Your lady is a freaking champ." Ray said. "She signaled me that she was about to make a move. It was a damn gutsy thing she did, given she had a gun at her head."

He stroked her hair back from her forehead. "She's a damn gutsy woman. Nobody has trouble seeing that but her."

The room filled with agreeing murmurs.

Wyatt looked up at Ray. "Thank you. When we realized one of the bad guys had slipped past us, I was terrified of the worst."

Ray shrugged. "There was never any danger of that

happening. If I hadn't taken Lexington out, Nadine would've found the strength to do it. I have no doubt about it."

Coming from Ray, that was high praise indeed. Not that Wyatt had any doubt about Nadine's strength.

Or that he was in love with her. Zero doubt about that either. They would try that conversation again when she wasn't in the middle of passing out.

But right now, he needed to get her to the hospital so they could reset her wrist and she wouldn't be in pain any longer. He planned to spend the rest of his life making sure she knew as little pain as possible.

He left the cabin and took Nadine to the hospital in Oak Creek, thankful when Zac's wife, Anne, was working a shift in the emergency room. Anne was patient and quietly reassuring as always and soon had Nadine's wrist back in place and pain under control.

"Zac mentioned you guys had some trouble out at Dorian's." Anne helped Nadine slip her arm into a sling. "He's on his way back there now that he's dropped Kendrick off at some safe house."

Nadine looked at him. "You need to get back there too, don't you?"

He really did, but her well-being came first. "They can handle it without me."

She smiled. "I'll be fine. You can drop me off at a hotel."

"Like hell I'm going to drop you off at a hotel. If you're going anywhere, it's to my place." Not that his place was the greatest—it was a studio apartment that he kept for when he was around Oak Creek. He spent so much time out of town on Linear business, he hadn't really put the effort toward creating a permanent space here.

Of course, now he realized that was because he'd been waiting to build his permanent place with Nadine—literally and figuratively.

"The ladies are at Charlie's. I'm heading there in a few minutes when my shift ends," Anne said. "Believe it or not, we don't sleep all that well when we know you guys are off doing something dangerous. Being with each other helps. Also, strength in numbers, just in case."

Wyatt nodded. Enemies of the Linear Tactical guys had tried to come at them more than once by attacking their women.

"We'd love to have Nadine with us." Anne reached out and squeezed Nadine's good hand. "Looks like she's one of us now anyway."

Wyatt couldn't deny that he loved the flush that colored Nadine's cheeks. Loved even more that she didn't deny what Anne had insinuated: Nadine was Wyatt's woman.

"Yes, she is." He turned to Nadine. "Are you okay going over there? I don't mind staying with you if that's what you prefer. Believe me, you're much better company than the guys."

"No, I'm okay. You go ahead and do what you need to do. As long as you promise to come get me when you're done."

He pulled her close and kissed her forehead. "There's zero chance of that not happening."

Anne expedited Nadine's hospital paperwork, and it wasn't long before Wyatt was driving Nadine to Finn and Charlie's house. Anne must have let Charlie know Nadine was coming because the tiny blond woman met them in the driveway. She shooed Wyatt away and welcomed Nadine inside, already asking if Nadine wanted a stiff drink to calm her nerves—insisting a deadly weapon to the head was a rite of passage nearly all of them had been through.

Wyatt left knowing the woman he loved was in good hands.

When he got back to Dorian and Ray's cabin, it was

obvious that the Linear reinforcements had been called in. Zac's vehicle was back, and it looked like Gabe Collingwood and Aiden Teague were both here to help out also.

And Gavin Zimmerman.

At any other time, Gavin would be the exact man Wyatt would want here in a situation like this. He, more than anyone, was levelheaded and strategic in his thinking. He also had contacts in law enforcement that would come in handy as they tried to come up with a plan about what to do with Lexington and the other bodies.

But Gavin was engaged to Lexi, the woman Nadine had been so surprised to see in town earlier today. The woman who was at least partially responsible for what had happened to Nadine and the scars she had because of it.

The Lexi everyone in Oak Creek knew was not the same person as the selfish Alexandra Adams Nadine had known for years on the set of *Day's End*. And Wyatt also knew Lexi had made her poor choices partially because of tragic things that had happened to her that Nadine wasn't aware of.

But if Nadine chose to never speak to Lexi again, Wyatt would support her. That was her decision because, unintended or not, Lexi's choices had almost gotten Nadine killed.

But supporting Nadine might put Wyatt at odds with one of his best friends. Because Gavin was always going to support Lexi, the woman he loved.

He and Gavin hadn't had a chance to talk since the news of Lexi's true identity had broken and Gavin and Lexi had gotten engaged. Wyatt hoped it wouldn't cause a problem now.

He entered the house and found his friends in Dorian's kitchen, serious looks on all their faces. Lexington's body had been removed. Zac was lying on the floor close to where

Lexington had died. He was holding a knife near his throat, so they were obviously reenacting what had happened.

That couldn't be good.

"I'm having difficulty picturing this exactly in my mind." Gavin's voice was gruff. "I need you to tell me again so it's absolutely clear. You can understand why this is of utmost importance."

Did Gavin think Ray had killed Lexington in cold blood? The man had had a gun to Nadine's head. Had broken into a cabin nobody in the world should know about. Gavin was a stickler for truth—as per his code name, *Redwood*—but this reenactment seemed a little over the top. Gavin was writing in a fucking spiral notebook, for God's sake. Like he was making a police report.

Wyatt looked at Dorian to make sure the man wasn't about to do something unthinkable. Because when it came to protecting Ray, damned near everything was *thinkable*. Dorian would take down even his closest friends if needed.

But to Wyatt's amazement, Dorian looked relatively calm. He nodded at Gavin. "No, I agree. The details are highly important in this situation."

Wyatt remained to the side since no one had said anything to him. Let them work through what they needed to.

"Okay, start from the beginning." Gavin said.

It looked like Dorian was playing Ray's role and Finn was playing Nadine. But then why would Zac, playing the dead Lexington, already be on the ground? He was about to point out the error when Finn spoke, looking deep into Dorian's eyes.

"You're the most amazing woman I've ever met."

What the—

Dorian took a step closer to Finn. "You said that to me

already." His voice was at least two octaves higher than usual.

Finn closed the rest of the distance between them. "Well, how about you're the most amazing woman I've ever met, and I'm in love with you."

Dorian clutched his wrist and pretended to fall to the floor. "Oh no . . ."

Wyatt had to smile as he rolled his eyes and stepped forward. "Okay, assholes. Ha ha."

"We're sure she passed out to get away from the declaration of love, not because of her dislocated wrist?" Gavin held his notebook up, pretending to write in it.

"Definitely," Finn responded.

Dorian nodded. "One hundred percent sure."

"No doubt about it," Zac said from the floor.

Wyatt threw his arms up and glared at Zac. "You weren't here!"

Everybody laughed. Dorian got up from the floor and slapped him on the shoulder. "Nadine doing all right?"

"Yeah. I took her to hang out with Charlie and the other women. She's in good hands. Get me up to date on the real issues here, not my love life."

Zac jumped up. "I got Kendrick to the safe house. He's contacting Ian DeRose since this is about Mosaic. Do you have any more info about where the drive actually came from?"

"No. Frank Jenkins mentioned that a guy named Claude gave it to him. Couldn't remember his last name, but thought it was something like 'seventy.'" Wyatt scrubbed a hand over his face. "Frank would've been able to tell us more but Mosaic had him killed."

Finn let out a curse. "Damned kid always wanted to be a hero."

Wyatt met the eyes of his friends. "Then let's make sure when this is said and done that he is one."

They all got back to work. Zac and Gavin were on their phones figuring out exactly how to handle the bodies. Nothing about what happened tonight could be processed as a crime scene here. Bringing outsiders, even law enforcement, into Dorian and Ray's safe haven was not an option. The bodies would have to be moved and "discovered" by Gavin somewhere else. He could then call his contacts in law enforcement.

Wyatt caught Gavin outside in between calls. "Thank you for doing this."

"It's my pleasure to do anything that will put Mosaic out of business for good. We've recently gotten Dorian and Ray back into the fold. I don't want to do anything that spooks them."

Wyatt looked back at the cabin. Ray had been antsy inside and had retreated to her bedroom. But then again, she'd just killed a man, so antsy was allowed. Plus, Ray pretty much always wanted to be alone, Dorian being the only exception.

But there was also something going on that Dorian and Ray weren't talking about. It had been evident all night. "Yeah, they've got other stuff on their minds too. Honestly, I'm not sure exactly what that is."

Gavin nodded. "Finn said something similar. But you know Dorian. He processes at his own speed. When he's ready to let us know what's going on, he will."

Wyatt's eyebrows drew together. "They've been through enough. I don't want them to fight a battle alone when we're right here, ready to help."

"Zac and Finn are going to tell Dorian the same thing." Gavin rubbed his eyes. "Also, not to make things awkward, but I'm really glad you and Nadine are together and she's here. I hope that doesn't cause a problem for you and me."

"Because of Lexi?"

"I love her, Wyatt. I love Oak Creek and you guys and my job at Linear, and I hope it doesn't come down to choosing, but if it does, I choose Lexi. There is no other option for me. If she has to leave, I'm going with her."

"I know." Wyatt did know because he felt the exact same way about Nadine.

"Lexi's not the same person she was when Nadine knew her. She would never do anything like that now."

Wyatt squeezed Gavin's shoulder. "I know. But Nadine is going to have to discover that for herself. If she wants to. I'm not going to force her."

"I understand."

"The rest we'll have to work out as we get to it. Right now, let's get Dorian's home back to a place he and Ray can live in without worry."

Gavin nodded. "Agreed. Deliver these bodies wherever they're going to need to go and get ready to help Ian DeRose take down Mosaic. I owe those bastards one. They tried to take Lexi earlier this year. Planned to use her as some sort of test subject for high-tech human trafficking. Chemical compounds that can be used for mind control."

"Shit. The more I learn about Mosaic, the worse it gets. And I have a feeling taking them down isn't going to be easy."

"But you getting the drive here in one piece? That was a huge start." Gavin reached out and squeezed Wyatt's shoulder. "It'll give Ian and his Zodiac Tactical team something to really work with for the first time."

Gavin stepped back with a smile. "And more importantly, it got you and Nadine together *finally*—who knows how long it would've taken you to make that move otherwise."

Wyatt breathed in the cool Wyoming air. Gavin was right. Regardless of what Kendrick got off of that computer drive, the most important thing was that when Wyatt left here, he'd be with Nadine. Holding her in his arms. Kissing all over that lush body.

The path had been unexpected, but it had led to her. That was all that mattered.

Chapter 19

The next two weeks went by in a blur. Wyatt kept Nadine sheltered from the action—and flying bullets—that went on as Kendrick tried to access the computer drive while Mosaic tried to make sure he didn't.

Nadine was more than okay with being sheltered. Not that the Linear team needed her help anyway. Those guys were a well-oiled machine.

And more than once, Wyatt's friends had taken time to point out that she'd done her part in this mission. An important part. That if she hadn't saved Wyatt in that hotel, the drive never would've made it into the right hands and Linear Tactical would be less one important member.

It was all but over now. Mosaic wasn't defeated, but Zodiac Tactical was in control now. Evidently, where Wyatt and the rest of Linear Tactical were more about teaching and training, Zodiac was made up of men who stayed on danger's front line. And now, Zodiac Tactical had someone undercover inside Mosaic.

Nadine was glad to have things getting back to normal, although *normal* was new and strange. She'd loved her two weeks here in Oak Creek. The women had welcomed her into their ranks immediately. She'd been kind of surprised until they'd all told her how much Wyatt had talked about her for the past two and a half years.

Evidently, for them, it had only been a matter of time until she'd shown up and joined them.

And she had loved being here in Wyatt's little apartment with him. She'd bought a laptop the second day and was successfully running her virtual assistant business from his couch. Canoodling with him there too. As well as on almost every surface in this place.

She'd gotten to tell him she loved him too without passing out. Everybody still teased her about that. And she loved it. Loved Wyatt to distraction.

Which would make the conversation they needed to have so hard.

In the past two weeks, she'd done as much as she could about getting things started on her house in Idaho. She'd hired a service to go in and salvage any personal effects they could—which hadn't been many.

The building itself was unsalvageable. Insurance would cover all of it, but everything would have to be replaced. The house would be rebuilt from the ground up.

It was time to go back there. She was going to need to be closer as construction commenced.

"I have to go back to Idaho."

It was after dinner when she finally got the nerve to say what she needed to, and they'd walked into town to get ice cream. She loved that it never once occurred to Wyatt that maybe a little less ice cream might be better for her figure.

He narrowed his eyes at her as he took a lick of his mint chocolate chip cone. "Why?"

"I need to get my life going in forward motion again. I need to find a builder and be closer to help supervise."

"Is that what you want?"

"I just think it's time."

It wasn't that she wanted to leave, but she couldn't keep staying in Wyatt's studio apartment. She loved being with him, loved him, but that wasn't a good space for both of them. Especially since she worked from home. It was crowded.

Their relationship had definitely not formed the traditional way. She knew they were going to be together, but she didn't want to rush or force anything.

"What if I knew a builder who would be perfect for you?"

"You know builders in Idaho?"

Another lick of the cone. "No. Actually, his contractor's license is for Wyoming. I was thinking . . . what if you built here?"

She stopped midbite of her fudge brownie cone. "Built here in Oak Creek?"

"Actually, I own a couple of acres a few miles out of town. I was thinking we might design a place together. One that has a great office for you. I know you need your space."

She wasn't exactly sure what he was asking her. Was he saying he wanted her to move here so they wouldn't have to date long-distance? Was he saying he wanted them to move in together? Or was he only offering to help her design a place?

"Would . . . would there be other rooms in this house?"

He nodded. "A very large master bedroom, with a fire-place next to huge windows that have breathtaking views."

That still didn't help her. Was she going to have to ask him outright what this conversation meant for their relation-ship? "And other rooms? Would we need other rooms?"

He gave her a lopsided grin. "Of course, silly. A kitchen,

living room, dining room, bathrooms. Wouldn't be much of a house without those."

She narrowed her eyes. He was messing with her, he had to be. But he hadn't said anything that suggested they'd be in that house together. "Wyatt Highfield, what exactly are you saying to me?"

"Here, hold this for a second." He handed her his cone. "Don't eat it or else I get some of yours."

He reached into his pocket and she felt sure he was going for his phone, about to show her plans for the house he was talking about. Living here would be good. She liked it here, it was—

Her eyes bugged out as he got down on one knee in front of her, a ring held out, while she stood there holding two ice cream cones like an idiot.

"I'm hoping we can plan at least two bedrooms in our house for the kids we'll have. But we can always add on more if two kids aren't enough. Marry me, Nadine. I've known you're the one for me forever. I was waiting for you to get here."

She couldn't stop the smile that felt like it was going to split her face. "Yes. Yes, I love you, Wyatt."

Scattered applause broke out all around from people she hadn't realized were watching. Someone ran up and grabbed the cones from her.

Wyatt slipped the ring on her finger, then stood, wrapping his arms around her hips and lifting her until they were face-to-face so he could kiss her.

"I never would've lived it down if you passed out again, you know," he said against her lips.

She grinned. "You know it would've made a great story. They'd be acting it out for years."

❧

A COUPLE DAYS LATER, the guys left to drive down to Salt Lake City. Something about a strip club and declaring a fallen friend a hero.

Nadine was engaged to Wyatt. They'd spent almost every waking moment since celebrating that fact and each other's bodies. And talking about the house they were going to build.

But she'd known the whole time there was one more thing she had to work out before she could truly leave her past behind and walk into her future with him. The Linear guys being gone provided the perfect opportunity to handle it.

Talking to Alexandra Adams. Or Lexi Johnson, as everyone here knew her.

So she walked in the door of the Eagle's Nest, a small file in hand that she'd had overnighted to her.

"Sorry, we're not open for lunch service today, but we'll be opening for regular business hours at five if you want to come back then." Lexi was standing behind the bar with her back to the door so she didn't know it was Nadine who had entered.

Nadine watched her. Lexi's face may have changed due to the broken nose and cheekbone and some very artfully applied makeup, but the rest of her hadn't changed. The other woman still moved with a natural, sensual grace even while performing a mundane task like putting away glasses behind the bar. It was the sort of grace Nadine wouldn't be able to pull off if she practiced it.

When she had worked with Lexi on the set of *Day's End*, she'd always been a little jealous of how Lexi looked and moved and smiled and charmed without any sort of effort at all. None of those things had ever come easily for Nadine. She'd always been more clumsy and awkward.

"Actually, I'm not here for any sort of food. I wanted to see if we could talk."

Lexi stiffened at Nadine's words. She spun around slowly to face Nadine. "I was wondering when we would have our showdown. Not surprised you waited until the guys were out of town."

Nadine didn't deny it. Now was the best time without the guys here. Wyatt and Gavin were both too protective. They wouldn't have wanted to give the women the privacy they needed.

"Is that what this is? A showdown?"

Lexi put her hands on the bar. "I would've assumed that's what you would want. To run me out of town."

Nadine didn't move far from the door. "And if I did, wouldn't you argue that you were here first? That you've put down roots here by buying a bar and therefore if I don't like it, it's my own tough luck?"

Lexi grabbed the white towel that hung over her shoulder and wiped her hands with it before setting it on the bar. She came out from around it and walked toward Nadine.

She stopped about halfway, not seeming to know what to do. "No. No, I would definitely *not* say that. If you told me you were staking your claim here in Oak Creek with Wyatt and that I needed to leave, I—" The woman stopped and looked down at her feet for a long moment. "I would understand. After what I did to you, you pretty much get to demand whatever you want."

"What *you* did to me?"

"I almost got you killed. That was never my intention, but I'm sure that didn't matter to you much when you were sitting in the hospital for weeks trying to heal. I'm to blame."

No excuses. No putting it off on someone else. This

really was a different woman than the one Nadine had known on the film set.

She walked further inside. "I've become friends with Anne Mackay. She says the women in town sometimes come here for a girls' night out and that I should come with them next time."

Lexi rubbed the back of her neck. "I could schedule myself off work that night if that's what you want. I can understand how me being here would not make a girls' night out very fun. I pretty much am the only full-time employee of the bar, but if you let me know when you want to come, I'll make an effort not to be around." Lexi met Nadine's eyes. "That's if you'll let me stay in town at all."

If Nadine hadn't already forgiven the other woman, she would have now. And she couldn't kick her out of her home. "Anne also told me you saved her life the morning before her wedding."

Lexi shrugged. "I ran to get help. Hardly anything that could be called heroic."

That wasn't how Anne had explained it. Evidently, Lexi had put herself through some pretty agonizing miles to get the help Anne needed. There would've been a time when Alexandra would have made sure it was clear she was the heroine of the story as it was told. Yet another way she'd changed.

"I have scars," Nadine said.

Lexi flinched. "I know."

This had to be said. All of it. As brutal as it might be for both of them.

"I have the kind of scars that are frightening to look at. And until recently all they were was a reminder of the pain I'd gone through and my loss. Until Wyatt made me see that my scars are a badge of honor. Yes, they represent what I've gone through. But most importantly they represent that I survived. That I was strong enough to come out of it on the other side."

She took a step closer, pinning Lexi with her eyes. "Do you know who gave me the scars?"

"Me." Lexi's voice was a hoarse whisper.

Nadine placed the folder she'd brought into the bar with her on the table and walked over until she stood right in front of Lexi. The other woman flinched when Nadine put her hands on her shoulders. Like she expected a blow, but made no move to defend herself. Obviously, she thought whatever blow was coming was one she deserved.

"No."

"What?" Lexi blinked up at her.

"No, you are not responsible for my scars. The man who left me for dead is the one who is responsible."

"But I—"

"Alexandra. *Lexi*." Nadine squeezed her shoulders. "What you did was selfish and stupid. But you are not responsible for what happened to me or Chloe. Yes, Travis used the opening you provided. But if it hadn't been that night, it would've been another. He would have waited for a different opportunity. He was a psychopath."

Lexi shook her head. "But I—"

"You committed a crime, and you went to jail for it. And from what Wyatt has mentioned, you had reasons behind your behavior no one knew about. Makes it a little more understandable."

"I'm not sure I would feel that way if the roles were reversed." Lexi's chin dropped to her chest.

This woman had lost as much as Nadine had. Maybe she didn't have scars on the outside, but Lexi had lost everything and had been betrayed by people she should've been able to trust.

Nadine squeezed her shoulders again. "Because of you, I

met Wyatt, a man who looks at me like I'm the reason God created rainbows. Given everything I've been through, I'd do it all again if it meant I ended up here with him. So, in some ways, I'm thankful for what you did."

Lexi's face crumpled right before her eyes. Nadine pulled her into her arms, expecting her to reject the comfort or mock her for it. But she didn't. Lexi held on tight to Nadine.

"I'm so sorry. I'm so sorry. I found this wonderful town, and I have Gavin, and I'm so in love with him I don't know what to do with myself. He wants to marry me. But in the back of my mind every day has been the thought that I don't deserve this. That I don't deserve any happiness after what I did."

Nadine held her until the other woman stopped crying. Any last remnants of resentment or anger melted away with Lexi's tears. "It's time for both of us to put the past in the past. Move forward with the future."

Lexi wiped her eyes. "I don't think it's that easy."

"No, it's not. But we start here and find our way forward."

"Okay."

Nadine looked around. "I like your place. I have to admit, I never saw you as a bartender or waitress."

Lexi smiled and looked around with her. "I love it here. Honestly, I don't miss anything about acting. This is something I can build, grow. It's community."

"I'm glad you found a place for yourself. Somewhere you can fit in."

"Me too. Believe me, I never expected it."

Nadine stopped when she got to a group of pictures on the wall. Multiple images of different couples. Some she recognized—Zac and Anne, Finn and Charlie, Gavin and Lexi—many more she didn't. Older couples, younger couples.

It reminded Nadine of the other reason she was here. She turned back to Lexi. "It looks like I might owe you an apology too."

The face Lexi made was downright comical. "I highly doubt that."

"These pictures reminded me. I have a file of your stuff from the studio. Mostly pictures. It went into police evidence for a while, then somehow got sent to me before I quit the show."

"My stuff?"

"Technically it was your aunt and uncle's."

Lexi rolled her eyes. "If it was Nicholas and Cheryl's, then I definitely don't want it."

After what had happened, Nadine didn't blame Lexi for wanting nothing to do with them. She went and got the folder anyway.

"I think you'll want this. Evidently, they had it hidden away in your trailer. I think they forgot about it or maybe planned to manipulate you further with it."

"What?"

Nadine handed her the folder. Lexi opened it and sank to the floor, the contents in her hands. "I can't believe it. I thought all of them were gone."

The folder was filled with pictures of her parents. Some with Lexi in the shot, some without—but all of them filled with a love that was nearly tangible.

Nadine sat on the ground next to Lexi as she went through each one. Crying, laughing. "I can't believe it," she said again. "I didn't have any pictures of them—Cheryl and Nicholas deleted them all off my devices in a fit of rage one summer. There was nothing. And now . . ."

Lexi's eyes grew wide as she shook her head. "You could've destroyed them. Most people would've destroyed them, given what I did to you. Thank you, Nadine."

"I'm glad you have them."

Lexi picked up one of the photos and pinned it up on the wall with the other couples. "I always wondered if my parents had looked at each other with love. I was a teenager when they died—too wrapped up in my own drama to think about them that way."

Nadine joined her at the wall. "It looks like they did."

They stood studying the pictures for a long minute.

"Bring me one of you and Wyatt so we can add it to the board."

Nadine smiled. "I will. You know, I grew up in foster care. Never really had a family. And you lost yours as a teen. It never occurred to me that we were similar in that way."

Lexi slipped an arm around her. "But I think, in this town and with the men we've fallen in love with, we've both found our family now."

Nadine looked at all the couples in love on that wall and smiled. Being part of this was the last thing she'd ever expected and all she could've ever wanted.

Keep reading for the full three-part extended epilogue:
Part 1 – The News for Girl & Boy Riley (previously published as part of *Phoenix*)
Part 2 – The News for Quinn & Baby (previously published as part of *Baby*)
Part 3 - The News for Ray & Dorian (new)

Extended Epilogue Part 1 - The News for Girl & Boy Riley

Two and a half years after the end of Phoenix

Zac Mackay held a hammer in his hand and looked out at the newest addition to the Linear Tactical facility.

Not just the newest. The most important. Perhaps the greatest teaching tool that would ever be utilized here.

This was truly the way of the future. And it was finished. All the Linear Tactical guys had banded together to make sure this facility became operational today. The need for it was crucial.

There was no one else he'd rather have standing with him at this monumental moment than the men with him here now.

Finn. Aiden. Gavin. Wyatt. Dorian. The original group who'd served with him in the Special Forces and had been with him as the dream of Linear Tactical became a reality nearly eight years ago now.

His brothers-in-arms.

His *brothers*.

Dorian and Ray had been showing up in Oak Creek

more and more during the past year, Ray's features less pinched and tortured. Zac had actually heard the small woman laugh earlier today. Everyone had stopped for a second at the sound, then immediately gone back to work, not wanting to draw attention to it.

Nobody had needed to say what they'd all been thinking: that sound was beautiful.

Of course, Ray had multiple reasons to laugh now, didn't she? Or at least two very distinct ones. Nobody had seen that coming. But they'd all been thrilled when it had.

There were others here Zac hadn't served in the military with but who were just as important to him.

Gabriel Collingwood, the Navy SEAL who'd stormed into Oak Creek to follow his sister and then had stayed and made himself Jordan Reiss's personal guardian angel.

Jordan Reiss *Collingwood*. The two had gotten married on a beach in Maui almost two years ago now. Zac had been honored to be there watching them officially declare their love for and commitment to each other.

Zac's life would always be tied to Jordan's in tragedy, but the young woman deserved the happiness Gabriel was determined to give her.

Cade Conner was here too. The music superstar had been a huge financial part of Linear Tactical at its onset. His money hadn't been needed to fund this latest addition to the facility, but he'd still been here in support.

His wife, Peyton, and daughters, Jess and newborn Ella, had been touring with him the past two months. Jess was currently glued to Ethan's side, where she'd been since the minute she'd gotten home, the two of them inseparable as always, even as they got older.

Zac had laughed watching Finn nearly kill his preteen this summer. Ethan had never been one for moping but had seemed a little lost without Jess. Charlie had put him to work babysitting his younger siblings—Thomas, a toddler into everything, and Derek, almost six months old and just starting to scoot around. That had kept the kid busy.

Boy and Girl Riley were both here, although neither of them really had a stake in or use for this new facility. Phoenix was surprisingly terrible with tools, given his talents at so many other physical endeavors. But he'd still been here, lending support.

And he'd been by Girl Riley's side for every step in her MS journey. It had been a learning process for her as an individual, them as a couple, and all of them as extended family who'd wanted to help however they could.

Riley had learned to prevent her MS flare-ups as much as possible by figuring out her triggers and avoiding them when she could. An ever-changing blend of the correct amount of exercise, diet, rest, and medicine.

She'd gotten herself a T-shirt they all loved: *Multiple sclerosis . . . an autoimmune disease. Because the only thing strong enough to kick my ass is me.*

Girl Riley had taken an extended leave of absence from her job as an ER nurse last year so she could travel around with Phoenix while he filmed the first season of *Phoenix Rises*. She'd gotten quite a bit of screen time too. The Adventure Channel had expanded the program to include her MS struggles. She'd become a voice for millions of people suffering with similar autoimmune diseases: lupus, celiac, rheumatoid arthritis, and the many, many others that afflicted so many.

Phoenix had had to share the spotlight with another Phoenix rising.

Which he'd obviously been more than happy to do. Those Rileys were going to be fine.

"There's really only one word for this piece of beauty: *strategery*." Baby flipped a wrench around in his hand—

catching it in a way that spoke of years of familiarity. He also wouldn't be affected much by this newest Linear Tactical facility, but he'd not only helped build it, he and Kendrick had designed the damned thing.

Finn rolled his eyes. "I know your Ivy League wife doesn't let you get away with those sort of made-up words."

Baby grinned. "My gorgeous bride has no problem with whatever words I use as long as when we're in bed I—"

Finn covered Baby's mouth. "Please. I do not want to hear about your sex life."

Baby chuckled behind his brother's hand.

Gavin crossed his arms over his chest, just as proud as Zac. "Think of the skills that will be learned here. Leadership. Situational awareness. Agility. Downright survival."

Dorian reached down at his feet and grabbed a water bottle. "I never would've believed Linear would expand to include something like this."

Zac clapped his friend on the shoulder. "And here you are about to be the one to get the most use of it, Ghost."

"I thought I'd gotten my miracle the day I discovered Ray was alive." Dorian glanced over his shoulder at Ray who was talking to the other wives. Their thirteen-year-old son and eleven-year-old daughter were with her, running around with Ethan and Jess. "But those two . . . they completed me in a way I didn't know I was missing."

"Your family's story is not a traditional one, that's for sure." Gavin rubbed some grease off his hands. "But it's damned beautiful."

Dorian grinned and bumped fists with Kendrick, who was standing next to him. The most dire of circumstances had caused the two of them to grow closer in the past year. "You got that right."

Considering three out of the four members of Dorian's

family were legally dead in the eyes of the government, it was definitely nontraditional.

But the unadulterated love shining out of Dorian's eyes? Beautiful.

"Be a while before you'll be using this, Zac," Gavin said. "Me too, I guess. Although sooner if I can talk Lexi into it."

Zac looked at his own bride who was holding their six-month old daughter in a sling against her slender frame and talking to some of the other women.

Annie had known terror. First, when they'd gotten together four years ago, and then again with the almost tragedy on their wedding day eighteen months ago. It was still hard for Zac to let her out of his sight.

But through it all, Annie had never lost the quiet, gentle smile everyone loved about her.

Zac glanced at Noah Dempsey, also former military and Gavin's cousin, and gave the man a nod. If it weren't for him and his wife, Marilyn, Zac's world might've been crushed on his wedding day. Noah might be Gavin's family by blood, but he was Zac's family in every other way possible.

Zac was glad he and Marilyn and their two kids were here today. Glad all his extended family were here today for this important event.

"All right, guys, I think this is as complete as it's ever going to be," Zac announced. "It's time we opened this thing for business. I'm ready to see if it can live up to the hype."

"Hear, hear," Finn said. "Let a new generation of tactical awareness training begin."

∼

"Look at our big alpha men." Charlie laughed from where she was getting out food at the picnic tables with the wives and girlfriends.

The women all knew the men didn't expect them to stay over here for "women's work." But none of them was dumb enough to get in the guys' way when they were in full tactical mode. All the women had known they were falling in love with warriors from the beginning.

Not that they could've stopped themselves from falling if they'd wanted to.

Violet grabbed baby Derek so Charlie could move more easily. "I know. Standing around congratulating themselves like they created some sort of huge training facility rather than a playground."

Ray began opening bags of chips and laid them on the table. "You know they've been planning that thing down to the last detail. It's all Dorian has been talking about for weeks. He and Theo met with Baby about the design more than once."

Ray glowed.

Annie was honestly thrilled to have her here talking—to have her here at all interacting with people would've been enough. But Ray was so much more than talking. She was smiling and laughing. She'd come so far from those heart-breaking, noise-reducing headphones she'd covered her ears with for so long.

Ray's life hadn't been easy or traditional. No one should be surprised that her journey into motherhood had been unique too.

She'd been thrust into it—sink or swim.

She'd swum. Amazingly well, she'd swum.

Theo and Savannah were her children—it was obvious in every glance and touch. Maybe not by blood, but in every way that mattered. The kids adored her and Dorian also.

A family of survivors, all willing to protect each other no matter what.

The results of Ray's medical tests in a file on her desk at

the hospital weighed heavily on Annie's mind. Ray had been through enough, and Annie hated to have to give her difficult news.

Annie had hard news for both Ray and Baby's new wife, Quinn.

The talks were going to be hard. Requiring life-changing decisions from both women and their husbands. The knowledge of it weighed on Annie.

But this wasn't the place or time to discuss it. This was a time for celebration and laughter.

Case in point, all the kids cheering and running toward the new playground now that the men had deemed it ready. Ethan and Jess ran with Theo and Savannah, slowing to let two-year-old Thomas run with them. Noah and Marilyn's kids, Sam and Eva, were right there in the fray too, always welcome when they were in town.

Annie kissed the top of Becky's head in the sling at her chest. She hated the choices her friends were going to have to make but was selfishly thankful she didn't have to make them herself.

Becky shifted and opened her big blue eyes. Zac's eyes. "Hi, baby girl," Annie whispered.

"Are you really going to make me wait until next week to come into your office and talk about the test results?" Girl Riley walked over, then reached down and kissed the soft fuzz on Becky's head before knocking Annie's hips with her own.

"It's nothing bad, I promise." The least of the concerning news she needed to give.

"Then tell me now. Is it a new MS breakthrough somewhere? I promise I won't get my hopes up because you tell me there's a new type of medicine. I know not every MS medical breakthrough will benefit me."

Annie smiled at her friend. Riley had been doing so well

with her day-to-day health challenges. It hadn't been easy, but Mrs. Riley Harrison was a trouper, especially with Mr. Riley Harrison right beside her every step of the way.

"Just come in next week. We don't need to get into it here."

Riley's eyes narrowed. "Now you've really got my attention. What's going on?"

Annie shook her head. "Seriously, it's not—"

"Look, spit it out. I can take it. Was it something with my latest MRI?"

Riley was bracing herself for bad news. Damn it, this wasn't what Annie had been trying to do. "No, not at all. I promise." She touched Riley's arm. "We'll talk about it in the office on Monday."

"It's MS related. Damn it, I knew it. Knew things had been going too good lately. I knew if—"

"You're pregnant, Riley."

"—I changed my meds I . . ." Riley's eyes widened, and words trailed off. "What?"

"You're going to have a baby," Annie whispered. Nobody was really listening to their conversation, but Annie didn't want to announce it.

Riley shook her head and backed up, stumbling a bit and stretching her hand back to catch herself on the nearby picnic table.

"Wildfire!" Boy Riley yelled, aware as always of what was going on with his wife. "Clumsy or medical?"

Annie knew that was their code, one Girl Riley responded very well to. She didn't want every mishap she had to automatically be lumped under MS. Boy Riley always asked—knew that fighting her own battles was important to her.

Girl Riley turned to look at her husband, then back at Annie. "Are you sure?"

Annie squeezed her hand. "Yes. And before you ask, no, there shouldn't be any complications related to MS. As a matter of fact, many women report fewer flare-ups while being pregnant."

"Wildfire?" Boy Riley jogged over to them. "You've got me a little worried. Clumsy or medical, sweetheart?"

Girl Riley turned toward him. "Neither. Pregnant."

Now it was the great Phoenix's turn to stumble a little. "*Pregnant?*"

Girl Riley nodded.

He turned to Annie. "For real? Is it safe? Okay?"

"Yes. It's absolutely safe and okay. No more risk than any other pregnancy."

Annie stepped out of the way as Phoenix went and knelt in front of his wife and tenderly kissed her still-flat belly. "We're going to have a baby, Wildfire."

She trailed her fingers through his hair. "Like that vision I had in our house."

He stood up and turned back to the guys. "We're going to have a baby!" He picked Riley up and spun her around. "I'm going to be a dad."

"Please don't name the kid Riley," Kendrick yelled. "Your names are confusing enough as it is."

Everyone laughed and soon hugs were being shared all around. The kids enjoyed the new playground and the parents got out the rest of the food and drinks to make the most of this gorgeous Wyoming summer night.

"You okay?"

Annie leaned backward as Zac's strong, familiar arms came around her and Becky, pulling them both against him.

"Yes. I didn't mean to tell Riley about being pregnant. But she was worried it was something bad."

"Definitely not bad. The best. They're going to be a family."

She looked around at this crazy crowd—everyone passing around babies and food, laughing and talking all over each other. "We're already a family. It's just going to grow a little more."

She thought once more of the other news she still had to break. Riley had definitely been the easiest of the three. What was coming wouldn't be as easy. But this family would get through it the way they did everything.

Together.

(Keep reading for Part 2)

Part 2 - The News for Quinn & Baby

Two years after the end of Baby, *the day they built the playground*

The Linear Tactical picnic was breaking up by the time Quinn arrived. But she'd driven directly from the airport because she'd wanted to be here for her husband's big day. He'd been finalizing the plans for this playground for months. She knew that seeing it actually come to life would be a big thrill for him.

Two years of marriage and she still loved seeing him get excited about stuff like this.

She caught Finn and Charlie as they buckled their two younger kids into their car seats. Charlie grinned so hard, Quinn thought her face might split.

"You look pretty happy. What's going on?"

"Oh nothing." Charlie's smile didn't get any smaller. "Just a little announcement you missed."

"About the playground? Is everything okay with it?"

Quinn glanced in the direction of the elaborate play palace Baby had designed for all the kids who were now part of the Linear Tactical family. He'd worked so hard on it. She couldn't stand the thought that something had gone wrong, although looking at it now, it seemed to resemble the elaborate plans exactly as he'd drawn them up.

"Oh no," Finn said. "My brother designed a masterpiece, and the kids have already deemed him the most wonderful person to ever have graced the planet."

Quinn had to agree with the kids' good taste. "Then what is the big news?"

Charlie closed the car door. "We probably shouldn't tell you, but it's not like you're not going to hear it in a couple minutes anyway. You're going to be an aunt again."

Quinn's eyes got big, and she pulled Charlie in for a hug. "You're pregnant *again*? You guys are like rabbits! You do know how babies are made, right?"

Charlie laughed. "No, not me, dummy. Boy Riley and Girl Riley are having a baby. You're going to be an aunt on *that* side of the family."

"Are you serious?" Now it was Quinn's smile that threatened to split her face.

"Yup. Evidently it was a big surprise to them too. Anne knew and didn't plan to say anything here at the picnic, but then Girl Riley shook her down."

Quinn couldn't stop smiling. Her brother was going to be a *dad*. If he thought he'd done scary stuff up until now, Phoenix had another think coming.

"Those two left a while ago to process everything, but I'm sure you'll be getting a call from them soon." Finn smiled. "And as for us, I think three boys might be enough."

Charlie shot Quinn a look that said that particular topic was still open for debate as far as she was concerned. Quinn wasn't sure who would win that battle.

"Get over there and kiss my brother," Finn said. "He still doesn't like it when you're away."

She gave them a little wave and headed to where Baby

was talking to the only two remaining picnickers, Zac and Anne. She didn't like to be away from him either. She liked teaching the graduate-level workshop Harvard had offered, but traveling back to the East Coast twice a month, even in first-class on their dime, had become pretty exhausting.

Last month she'd been so tired, she'd barely recovered before it was time to turn around and fly back again.

She'd mentioned it to Anne in passing, and next thing she knew, she'd been bullied into coming into the hospital and having blood work done. Anne was concerned Quinn might be anemic.

Maybe some iron shots would help her feel better, because she had to admit she felt like crap. She didn't want to let Baby know, but she was tired all the time.

She was forty-one years old. Her husband had turned thirty a couple months ago. Telling him she *already* couldn't keep up with him did not bode well for their future. She thought she'd gotten past the age-gap fears that had nested inside her brain, but evidently not.

Zac said something to Baby that made him cross his arms over his chest and nod. They both looked at the new playground equipment, and Baby saw her walking toward him.

The smile that lit his gorgeous face was so big that every concern she had about any of their differences floated away.

More than three years together, and he still looked at her like she lit up his very world. She understood that because she felt the exact same way.

As soon as she reached his side, he yanked her against his chest and kissed her as if there were nobody else around.

"Baby." She laughed when she could finally catch her breath and pushed at his muscled chest.

"Hey, Cupcake. You're home early. Thank goodness."

"I wanted to see your masterpiece. I'm sorry I missed the kids playing on it."

"Oh, there will be plenty of kids to watch playing on it in the future, don't you worry."

"Including my brother and Girl Riley's new little one, so I hear."

"Charlie can't keep a secret to save her life." Anne laughed and rolled her eyes. "Although, I guess neither can I since Riley somehow maneuvered me into telling her private news in the middle of the picnic."

"Pregnancy is happy news." Zac wrapped an arm around Anne, looking at their infant daughter, Becky, sleeping in the carrier on the table. "Gives them more to celebrate."

"Yeah, I was happy to give some good news. It doesn't always end up that way." Anne shot a look at Quinn, then looked away quickly.

Baby didn't notice the look, thankfully; Quinn hadn't mentioned her medical appointment to him.

But Quinn noticed.

The guys walked over to discuss something about the playground, and she knew she had to pull a Riley and get Anne to spill more news.

"Are you going to tell me what that look was about?" Quinn said as soon as the guys were out of earshot.

Anne busied herself tucking a blanket in around her daughter.

"Anne, it's okay to tell me. Whatever it is, I'd rather face it straight on."

Anne still didn't turn. "How are you feeling? Still tired?"

Quinn closed her eyes for a second. There *was* something wrong with her health. If nothing was wrong, Anne wouldn't have led with that.

"You know if you don't tell me, I'm going to go home

and research all the possibilities. I trust your medical degree more than what some random stranger is going to tell me on the internet."

Anne finally turned to face her. The worried look in the quiet woman's eyes did not reassure Quinn. "It's late. You've traveled clear across the country. Why don't you and Baby come in on Monday morning to see me. We can talk."

She went back to the unnecessary tucking of the blanket. Did Anne really not understand that at this point her silence was making it worse?

Quinn crept to where little Becky slept peacefully. She and Baby had tried to get pregnant when they'd first gotten married, since they'd known the window of opportunity was narrow. But it hadn't worked out for them. After Theo and Savannah had come into Dorian and Ray's lives, she and Baby had decided they'd definitely like to adopt, although not the same way as the Lindstrom family.

Nobody would ever adopt the way they had.

But Quinn and Baby had so much love in their hearts to offer a child that adoption had seemed like a wonderful option. Maybe older kids. Maybe foster to adopt.

Quinn had made her peace with never having a biological child. She was fine with it. But she'd never considered that maybe she was terminally ill or something and now *any* sort of family was out of the question.

She grabbed Anne's hand on the baby carrier. "I'm not trying to wreck your weekend, Anne, really. But I want to know if I need to prepare myself, and Baby, for the worst."

"I knew something was wrong."

Quinn spun around at Baby's words, not having realized the guys had walked back over.

His green eyes were filled with worry. "I know you've been trying to hide it, but I could tell. You've been exhausted all the time and quiet. I thought you were sad. I thought maybe being out at Harvard made you realize how much you missed it. But are you saying there's something physically wrong?"

Quinn should've known he would notice. He noticed everything about her—wasn't that one of the reasons she loved him so much?

She turned back to Anne. "I don't know if there's something physically wrong with me. Anne and I thought maybe I was anemic, so I had some blood work done last week."

Anne rubbed her eyes with her thumb and forefinger. "Actually, it ends up you are a little anemic. We need to get you on some iron."

"But there's more," she and Baby said at the same time.

She looked at him, their hands instinctively seeking each other. She stepped toward him until their hands grasped each other.

Whatever this was, they would handle it the way they had learned how to handle everything life threw at them: *together*.

He gave her a little nod that let her know he was thinking the same thing. She let go of his hand and wrapped an arm around his waist as his arm came around her shoulders.

"Tell us." Together, again.

"Fine." Anne let out a breath and took a step closer. "But I want you to listen to everything I have to say before you react."

This had to be bad. Baby's hand squeezed her shoulder.

"Okay," she whispered.

"Girl Riley isn't the only one who's pregnant."

Quinn waited for the rest of the statement, but it didn't come.

Shock flooded her system. Wait—

"Me?" Her gaze flew to Baby, then back to Anne. "I thought you told me I couldn't get pregnant anymore."

Anne shook her head. "No, I said that the older you got, the fewer eggs you release each month, which of course lessened your chance of becoming pregnant, and that you should make sure you'd come to terms with that."

Quinn could hardly process what she was hearing. She leaned into Baby, staring up at him. Her rock. The one who helped her make sense of anything she couldn't seem to understand. "I'm pregnant?"

But there were still shadows in his eyes. He was remembering the rest of what Anne had said. That they had to get *all* the news before they reacted.

Right. She grabbed a fistful of Baby's shirt. "Is the fetus okay?"

"Is Quinn okay?" Baby asked.

Anne gave them a tight smile. "Yes. You're around thirteen weeks pregnant, so the good news is that you're past the normal miscarriage stage. But getting pregnant at your age is considered high-risk. We'll have to monitor you closely. Weekly visits. There are factors we'll want to take into consideration—gestational diabetes, high blood pressure, which can lead to preeclampsia."

High-risk. Okay, Quinn could handle that.

"You also need to know that women who get pregnant after the age of forty, especially for the first time, run a higher risk of having a child born with Down syndrome. When we ran your blood, it was standard practice to check certain proteins. Those levels weren't normal."

Quinn wasn't sure how she was supposed to react. "Does that definitely mean the baby has Down syndrome?"

Anne shook her head emphatically. "No, but it means the chance is higher."

"What does that mean?" Baby asked. "I mean, I know what Down syndrome is, but what does it mean? Will the baby die?"

Anne shook her head emphatically again. "*No.* No, all it means is you might have a kid with an extra chromosome. He or she will still be beautiful. Still be your child. Just might need some extra help in life."

"I know all about needing a little extra help, and Quinn knows all about giving it." He squeezed her shoulder.

Quinn nodded slowly. This wasn't nearly the same thing. "So, what do we need to do?"

"On Monday, I'd like you to come in so we can get you assigned to an OB-GYN. We'll do a normal prenatal workup. I can answer any questions you have." Anne grabbed both their hands. "In two weeks, we can do an amniocentesis. That's a procedure that will let you know more definitively whether the baby has Down syndrome."

Quinn squeezed Anne's fingers. "Will the baby having Down syndrome or not make any difference in my pregnancy?"

"No, not at all. Your pregnancy will be completely normal, subject to all the good and bad parts of a pregnancy. Your baby will be born and cry and coo and poop like every other baby regardless of whether he or she has Down syndrome or not."

"Then why have the test?" Baby asked. "Is there anything in particular we need to prepare for that the results will give us?"

Anne pressed her lips together. "No. Generally, the test is primarily for your peace of mind, and in case you decided you didn't want to go through with the pregnancy."

Quinn reached out to pull Anne into a hug. "Thank you. You've carried a heavy burden this weekend, but I appreciate you telling us now rather than making us wait."

"I want you to know that I support you no matter what you decide. And no one else in Oak Creek will know you're pregnant unless you decide to tell them. They never need to know you were ever pregnant at all."

Quinn, a little numb, nodded and grabbed Baby's hand as they both turned to walk toward the car. She put her other hand on her belly.

She was *pregnant*.

∼

Two weeks later

Baby curled his hand over his beloved sleeping wife's belly. She was fifteen weeks pregnant. According to the books he'd read, books she'd helped teach him to read two years ago, the fetus was roughly the size of an orange.

Her belly was gently rounded, soft, not much different than the way it had always been. The way he loved.

She'd been to see Anne three times since the day they'd found out she was pregnant. According to the doctor, everything about the pregnancy seemed fine, and Anne had referred her to an OB-GYN. Both doctors had said Quinn's hCG levels were right on target for Quinn's due date.

Her due date if she decided to carry the pregnancy to term.

Today was the day of the amniocentesis. Quinn probably knew more about that test than most doctors did. She'd studied it, studied Down syndrome, looked at all the ways their lives would change if their child was afflicted.

Baby was doing his best to support Quinn in whatever way he could. He knew how her mind worked. Knew she needed to surround herself with as much information as possible in order to make a decision. To an outsider, it might look cold and calculating to consider their unborn child with such deliberate objectivity. Trying to decide the best course of action.

Baby already knew the best course of action. He'd known it the moment Anne had said Quinn was pregnant. The only thing that would have made a difference for him was if Anne had said the baby was jeopardizing Quinn's life.

He reached down and whispered next to Quinn's belly, "But you're not, are you, tiny person?"

The child growing inside her was a part of both of them. Baby didn't care how many extra chromosomes the little one had. He was prepared from the first moment to welcome him or her into their family.

But he knew his big-brained wife needed to work things through in her own way. And if she decided a child with this sort of special needs was more than she could handle . . .

Well, then she was about to be surprised by how good of an academic he'd become. He had a plan. A way to assure Quinn that she would get the support she needed no matter what their child needed. He had charts and graphs and statistics, but most of all, he was ready to prove to her that she would be a wonderful mother no matter what.

And she would be.

No matter what.

Her fingers slipped into his hair, scratching gently. "What you doing down there?"

He kissed her belly, then slid up until he could kiss her lips.

"I wanted to see if I could tell any difference. Still looks just as beautiful to me."

"About the test today . . ."

He waited, then waited some more, but she never finished. "We face it together, no matter what." He kissed her again. "Together."

"I . . ."

She trailed off again. Again he waited, but she never finished. He kissed her once more. "You better hit the shower. We've got to leave in an hour."

"Roger."

He went into the kitchen to make his coffee and her decaffeinated tea. He'd already finished his entire first mug; she was still in the shower.

She never took this long. He glanced at the clock. They were supposed to leave in a little more than thirty minutes. There was no way she was going to have time to get her hair up into her proper teaching/appointment bun—he'd given up on trying to talk her out of that as long as she kept her hair down and loose at home.

"What the heck is she doing?" he asked Grizzly. The dog stared at him with the same bored acceptance he always did.

Still more water. Maybe something was really wrong. He dropped the coffee cup onto the table with a thud and rushed to the shower.

Quinn was sitting on the shower floor, arms wrapped around her knees, crying.

He got in fully clothed and turned off the water. He sat down next to her, hauling her up into his lap.

"Cupcake, come on. Don't cry." He smoothed her hair down, pushing it back from her face.

"I need to tell you something," she finally got out after a few shuddery breaths.

Baby closed his eyes. He had a feeling he knew what she was going to say. And maybe he'd been wrong in what he'd been thinking. Maybe if she really didn't feel like she could handle a child with special needs, he shouldn't push it. Adoption was still just as great an option as a biological child.

If this child wasn't meant to be, then he would trust they would have children other ways.

He remembered that trip he'd taken to Cambridge to

convince her that they belonged together. He'd been prepared to leave everything behind here in Oak Creek because he'd never wanted her to feel trapped by the choices she'd made to be with him.

That was still true in the choices they'd made to start a family.

"What do you need to tell me, Cupcake?"

"I'm afraid you'll think I'm being unreasonable, but I've made up my mind about my pregnancy."

He closed his eyes and rested his lips against the top of her head. "Tell me."

"I know you want me to have the amniocentesis today, but I don't want to have it."

His eyes flew open. "What?"

"There's some risk of miscarriage from the test itself, and I don't want to take that chance."

"But it's the best way to know whether the baby has Down syndrome or not."

"I don't care. I know you want me to have it but—"

He shifted her so he could see her eyes, ignoring the fact that they both resembled drowned rats. He trailed a thumb under one of those brown eyes that had gutted him from the very beginning, now rimmed red from crying. "I wanted the test so you would have all the information, Cupcake. I know how your brain works. If our child has Down syndrome . . ."

She shrugged. "Then he or she has Down syndrome. It doesn't change anything. It's still our child and will be loved no matter what. I want *this* baby. I'm not afraid."

He caressed her belly. "Me neither. No matter what." They would face whatever the future brought *together*.

She smiled. "Shower with me, then let's go into town to eat. I'm starved. It's time to start telling everyone that Baby is going to have a baby."

Part 3 - The News for Ray & Dorian

Twenty-two months after the end of Scout, *the day they built the playground*

Anne hummed softly in the rocking chair, holding her daughter close. Becky had fallen asleep fifteen minutes ago, but Anne hadn't wanted to put her down even though it was time to go get ready for her overnight shift at the hospital.

"You know, a doctor once told me that you shouldn't let a baby get used to falling asleep in your arms, especially in a rocking chair. That it's important for babies to learn how to go to sleep in their crib."

Her husband lounged in the doorway, arms crossed over his chest in a way that still made her heart flutter all these years later. His sexy voice was low, maybe to make sure he didn't wake their daughter, but maybe because he knew what his low voice did to her.

"I'm pretty sure the doctor who said that only did so because she wanted to be the one to hold and rock the baby at the time."

Zac gave her that smile that did even more to her insides. "Do you want to call in and miss your shift tonight? You've already had a pretty full day of diagnosing."

Neither of which she'd been planning on as the guys had built the new playground, but somehow it had happened anyway. And there was still one more diagnosis she needed to give another friend. To Ray. And it would be the hardest news of all.

That aching feeling in her chest was back, and no amount of rocking her sweet daughter could take it away. Anne hated to add to the weight Ray already carried, especially now, since she was so happy with her new family.

"Hey." Zac moved in from the doorway and picked her and Becky up as if they weighed nothing, sat down in the chair, and lowered them into his lap. The baby slept soundly on. "What's going on?"

"I'm okay. It's some bad news for Ray. I'm going to need to get her into the office soon."

"Really bad news?" She knew he wouldn't ask her for specifics, putting her in a position where she had to violate privacy laws. But they all knew if something bad happened to Ray that it was going to take the entire Linear team to help Dorian keep it together. The two of them had already been through so much. Way too much.

"Not the worst." It was bad, but not the worst. She tried to remind herself of the motto the Linear guys lived by: *survival was the most important thing.* So no, this was not the worst.

"I'm glad to hear that, although I know there's still plenty of other bad out there."

Anne snuggled into Zac's chest, drawing from his strength like she always had. It wasn't the worst. Ray would survive. Survival was the most important thing.

Anne hoped it wouldn't put out the light they'd all been

so happy to see in Ray's eyes.

Anne showed up for work on time, but only barely. The overnight shift would be brutal after today's emotional upheaval with Girl Riley and Quinn.

Which was why she was so surprised to see Riley in the emergency room in her nursing scrubs.

"What are you doing here?" Anne asked as she pulled her friend in for a hug. Riley had taken a leave of absence from her nursing job partially to deal with her multiple sclerosis diagnosis, but also to travel the world with her famous husband and be part of his Adventure Channel reality television show, *Phoenix Rises*.

Anne especially hadn't expected to see Riley here given the fact she'd found out today she was pregnant.

"I was already on the schedule. Hospital administrators have agreed to let me work the shifts I need to keep my licensing current."

"Did that have to be today? Shouldn't you be out celebrating?"

Riley rolled her eyes. "Believe me, Boy Riley and I have already celebrated. But then he was starting to get that overprotective look in his eye. Pregnancy evidently is going to throw us back into that stage of our relationship where he watches me like a hawk, afraid I might keel over at any moment. So I thought it would set a good precedent to work the shift I was scheduled."

Anne smiled. "Good for you. I'm glad to have you on the floor, just like old times. I've got to handle some paperwork in my office, then I'll be back out to chat. Hopefully, tonight will be slow."

Anne checked in at the nurses' station for the ER to

make sure nothing needed her immediate attention, then headed back to her office. Ray was still weighing heavily on her mind. The test results meant more tests were needed and waiting would only make the situation worse. She'd call Ray in the morning and arrange something that could work for the other woman.

Ray wouldn't casually walk through the front doors of the hospital and submit for testing. Understandable, since according to the government the woman was dead. She didn't want to be in the system in any way.

Anne unlocked her office door, bypassed the switch for the jarring florescent light, and dumped her bag and files on the desk before turning on the small desk lamp.

She'd been able to take Ray's blood sample and perform the initial exam at her house, but she would need specialized equipment for the next tests. She didn't have an ult—

"Do you mind if we leave the big light off?"

Anne's head jerked up. Ray stood in the back corner of her office, hidden mostly by shadow.

Anne clutched her heart and took a shaky breath. "I suppose it's a good thing we're in a hospital so that they can treat me quickly if I'm having a heart attack."

"Sorry." Ray gave her a wry smile. "I thought it was best if I didn't announce my presence here."

Anne didn't ask Ray how she'd gotten into her office or the hospital undetected. Honestly, she didn't want to know.

"You have my blood test results back."

It wasn't a question. *This*, Anne did want to know how Ray had found out. She raised an eyebrow. "If I ask you how you know that, will you tell me? I didn't use your name because I didn't want you to end up in the system."

Ray's eyes pinned hers without so much as a flinch. "I broke into your house, recorded the number you used to put my blood into the system, then hacked into the hospital system to plant an alarm to let me know when the results came back."

Anne wasn't sure exactly what she was supposed to say to that. Ray's actions violated all sorts of laws and privacy policies, and she'd *broken into* her and Zac's house.

She took a breath. That wasn't what was important right now. Ray was here in the hospital. Anne needed to take advantage of that.

"Did you look at the test results?" The initial results were pretty clear and wouldn't require any sort of medical degree to interpret. Would actually seem positive at first glance.

"No. Dorian wouldn't let me."

"Good for Dorian. Googling results of a medical test is not the same as a professional medical opinion."

"But you did find something." Ray crossed her arms over her chest.

"Yes."

"Is it bad?"

"Possibly. Honestly . . . probably. It depends on your answer to this question: how much pain are you in?"

How much pain was she in?

That was a loaded question if Ray had ever heard one. Pain was such a relative thing.

"I'm not sure exactly how to answer the question," she finally told Anne.

She doubted the other woman understood the degree of trust Ray was placing in her by showing up here at all. Ray's life had changed so much in the past two years, in ways she'd never dreamed of and definitely didn't deserve. But that didn't mean that trust came easy. Shutting herself in a room with another person and only one exit was more than Ray was willing to do with 99.999 percent of the rest of the population.

The only three people she trusted to that degree without question weren't here. They were at home, sleeping, not aware she wasn't in the house with them.

Anne studied her. "We ask people to rate their pain on a scale of one to ten. One being—"

"I understand the pain scale." Ray just wasn't sure how to rate herself on it.

Given that she'd been trained to break her own bones without giving away to captors that she felt anything and had been regularly tortured as part of her own training . . . pain was relative.

But yes, she could admit, at least to herself, that she was in pain. And it had been getting worse. Dorian had noticed it and her dizziness a few days ago. It was why he'd insisted she go to see Anne.

"Yes," she finally said. "I have some pain."

"I'm going to assume that coming from you that admission holds a lot more weight."

"Maybe. But it's tolerable, so I don't want to focus on that. I want to skip straight to what you found in the test results. You know some of what Project Crypt did to me.. We're not sure what the long-term effects from that might be. A predisposition toward cancer. Tumors, maybe. Dorian and I are both concerned it could be something potentially deadly so—"

"You're pregnant."

There weren't many things that could catch Ray off guard, but those words coming from Anne's mouth definitely did.

As always, she recovered quickly. "That's not possible. I had my tubes tied years ago." When she found out her own body was being used for missions she had no control over.

"Tubal ligation is highly effective, but not one hundred percent." Anne held out a hand, features pinched. "The problem is, most pregnancies that occur after tubal ligation are ectopic pregnancies. I'm pretty sure that's what has happened to you. It's why you're in pain."

"Right."

Pregnant.

"Ray, it's almost definitely an ectopic pregnancy—one that's outside of the uterus. In most cases, it's in the fallopian tubes. I need to do an ultrasound to be sure. It's not a viable pregnancy."

"Do you believe in miracles, Anne?"

"Ray." Anne rubbed her eyes. "I'm sorry, but in an ectopic pregnancy, the fetus can't survive. It's . . . not a miracle."

The gentle, kind doctor didn't understand. "But do you believe in them?"

Anne let out a sigh. "Yes, I do believe in miracles."

The woman was about to launch into the medical facts about this doomed pregnancy again, but Ray held out a hand to stop her. "I have a man who forgave me for the unthinkable and saved me in every way a person could be saved. He loves me to distraction. That is a miracle."

Anne nodded. "Love is the most wonderful kind of miracle."

Ray turned to glance at the bookshelf behind her, then back at Anne. "I have two children who call me Mom. Wonderful children who I can't help but believe that fate or God or the universe—whatever you want to call it—brought directly to me. Literally dropped them on my doorstep. Also a miracle."

Anne nodded. "Yes."

She walked forward so she was standing directly in front of Anne's desk. The woman still looked so worried, like this news was going to break Ray in some way. "I understand this pregnancy is not viable. I understand what an ectopic pregnancy is, and it's okay. I have my miracles. I have more miracles than someone like me ever deserved. I came here today because I thought you were going to tell me I was dying. I thought you were going to tell me that I didn't get much more time with my miracles. But that's not what you're saying, so I'm okay. You do whatever it is you need to do so that I can get home to my miracles, and I'm going to be fine."

A burst of pain shot through her midsection, but she was careful to hide it. She was so damned relieved to know that this wasn't the worst.

Another miracle.

The look of sheer relief on Anne's face was almost comical. The woman was so sweet and kind she hadn't wanted to deliver bad news, even relatively minor bad news, considering Ray had long ago made peace with the fact that she'd never have biological children.

And yet she was still a mother.

"Okay." Anne smiled. "While you're here, let me go ahead and do the ultrasound, see where the ectopic pregnancy is and how we need to proceed."

When Ray nodded, Anne didn't waste any time and led her out of the office and to a private room in the hospital's emergency section. She kept talking the whole time.

"If you were in pain enough to admit it and come see me for testing, you're probably pretty close to a rupture. I can pull some strings and we can try to do the surgery tomorrow. We'll get Neo and Kendrick on it to make sure there's no electronic trace of you being here."

"Okay." The sooner all of this could be behind them, the better. She didn't want to worry Dorian and the kids, and she appreciated that Anne took her need for absolute secrecy so seriously.

Anne grabbed her hand and gave it a gentle squeeze. "We're going to take care of you, Ray. I promise."

Ray squeezed back. This woman was family. And family was formed in all different ways, Ray knew that from experience.

She got undressed from the waist down so Anne could do the ultrasound. She hadn't been expecting an OB-GYN-type test when she'd arrived here tonight.

"I'm calling in Girl Riley. She happens to be on shift here tonight, and she can help me cover our tracks. Is that okay?"

"Sure. I'm surprised she's here, given her news today."

"Me too. Evidently Boy Riley was being a little too overprotective, and she needed some space."

Girl Riley arrived a couple minutes after Anne texted her. She was surprised but happy to see Ray, and Anne quickly apprised her of the situation.

Riley squeezed her hand like Anne had done. A show of support, of concern. "I'm so sorry, Ray."

"Thank you. But I've got my miracles at home, so it's going to be fine. And I'm excited for you and Boy Riley."

Anne was quick and efficient with the transvaginal ultrasound and within a few minutes was pointing out the gestational sac in one of her fallopian tubes on the screen.

Riley was shaking her head. "Holy shit, Ray. Aren't you in pain?"

"It's tolerable." Actually it hurt like hell, but that would be okay.

"See how this is inflamed? We need to get her to surgery, stat. That's probably not going to wait till tomorrow to rupture."

Ray had to grit her teeth to breathe evenly through the

pain now. "Call Dorian. Tell him what's going on. Get Kendrick on it."

"Jesus, Anne, do you see that?" Riley pointed to something on the monitor, but Ray was having trouble focusing on it. She was dizzy, everything was tilting.

And fuck, the pain . . .

"Ray . . . Oh God . . . Heterotopic pregnancy . . . Ray?"

Their voices faded in and out like their faces. She couldn't make out what they were saying, but she could see the fear in their eyes.

And then a ripping agony burst through her abdomen—one she couldn't keep silent through. She pulled her legs up to her chest and everything faded to black.

Dorian had awoken the moment Ray slipped out of bed; he always did. But he also knew that sometimes she needed to be alone to battle whatever demons came calling. More importantly, he knew she was strong enough to do it. To battle every demon she had, plus any that might decide to come after him or the kids.

And he loved her for it.

She was concerned about whatever it was Anne was going to tell them about the medical test results. Honestly, he was concerned about it too. But whatever the results were, they would face it together.

A couple hours later, he cursed himself for being a fool when Ray still wasn't back in bed.

She'd gone to get the results of the test herself.

But goddamn it, he wasn't going to let her shoulder this alone. He'd long since accepted that protecting Ray from her enemies sometimes meant sometimes protecting her from herself.

He texted her, but she didn't respond, so he called Zac to see if she was at his house talking to Anne, despite the late hour. When Zac informed him Anne was working a shift at the hospital, Dorian had no doubt Ray had gone to talk to her there.

He left a note for the kids. He would probably be back before they woke up, but they were more than capable of taking care of themselves for a few hours if he wasn't.

Hell, his kids had proved themselves self-reliant for much longer than a couple of hours, and in much more dangerous circumstances. And at a younger age than any child should ever have to. So he wasn't worried about them.

He was halfway to the hospital when his phone rang. He expected it to be Ray, but it was Kendrick.

"Blaze, what's going on?"

"I need details, man. Girl Riley didn't tell me much, just that I needed to call you and get ready to electronically scrub Ray from the hospital."

Dorian slammed his foot on the gas pedal. "Why did she tell you that?"

"That's what I'm asking you!" Kendrick muttered something, then his voice rose again. "You're not at the hospital with them?"

"I'm on my way there now. Ray went to talk to Annie without telling me."

"Well, evidently that talk turned into emergency surgery."

Dorian's foot hit the gas harder. He didn't give a shit that he was taking these windy back roads way too fast. "What do you know?"

"Only that Anne was about to perform surgery, Riley was assisting, and they needed Neo and me to do our electronic voodoo to keep Ray out of the system."

"I'm ten minutes out from the hospital. I'll meet you

there. Call in everybody." He threw the phone on the seat next to him and gripped the steering wheel.

Ray would never have agreed to surgery without having Dorian there. Not because she was afraid to go under the knife, but because she would want to make sure the hospital was as secure as possible.

He had to focus on that—on making sure the hospital was as safe as possible for her. Because focusing on the possibility of losing Ray was enough to send a hardened former soldier like him into a panic.

Nothing in his life worked without her.

Fear locked his throat, choking out the air, with each unrecoverable minute it took to get to her.

He tore into the hospital parking lot and ran toward the door. Once inside, he slowed to a quick walk. The best thing he could do for Ray now was not bring any undue attention to him or her.

"Can I help you?"

He didn't recognize the nurse at the desk. He looked around but didn't recognize anyone who was currently working.

He wasn't sure what name or situation to ask for. Ray Lindstrom didn't technically exist. And if someone put the name Grace Brandt into the system, federal agents would be at the door to arrest her as soon as possible.

What would Annie have done in an emergency situation? She had to have entered some name.

"Lindstrom," He finally said. "I'm looking for—"

His phone beeped in his hand, a message from Kendrick. *Jennifer Williams.*

Two of the most common names in the country. Neo and Kendrick were already doing their magic in the hospital's computer system.

He gave a forced laugh. "Let me start again. I'm Dorian

Lindstrom. I'm looking for Jennifer Williams. She was taken in for surgery."

"Right." The nurse nodded, typing on her keyboard. "Our system has been acting up for the past few minutes, so I don't have any sort of update or information on her. But if you head straight back and take a left past the elevators, that's the surgery hall, where someone should be able to help you."

Dorian headed in that direction before she'd finished her sentence.

The nurse at the surgery hall desk seemed as confused as the first one he'd talked to. She couldn't find any information at all about Jennifer Williams except for the fact that she was in surgery and that Dr. Mackay was performing it.

Dorian told himself that was good. The less information available, the safer Ray was overall.

But the not knowing was killing him.

He wasn't sure what to do. Should he stay in case there was an update or Anne needed him for something? Should he move around the hospital, securing it as best he could? Or maybe work out as many exit points as possible if he had to get Ray out in a hurry under less than optimal circumstances?

He stared at the door leading to the surgery ward. The last time he'd felt this helpless was when he'd stood across a crowded café in Kabul, Afghanistan, and watched Ray die.

Yet she'd found her way back to him despite that. Despite it all.

They always found their way back to each other.

"Fight for me, Sunray. Fight for us."

If there was one thing he knew about that woman, it was that she was a fighter.

He wasn't sure how long he stood there in the waiting

room trying to figure out his best tactical option. A friendly hand on his shoulder dragged him back to the present.

Zac and Finn flanked him on either side.

"Any word?" Zac asked.

He shook his head. "All I know is that Jennifer Williams is in surgery. I don't know what for or how bad it is."

He didn't need to tell these two men that Ray would not be having surgery at all unless it was life-threatening.

"The team is on their way," Finn said. "Kendrick and Neo have a plan to help make sure the surgery draws very little attention. My understanding is that everybody we know is in on it."

Dorian nodded. "I'm not surprised those two came up with some elaborate scheme. That's their forte."

"Gabe is setting up surveillance so we have eyes on every entrance and exit in this place," Zac said. "All your woman has to do is get through this. We'll make sure she's safe from everything else."

"And me? What do I do?" Dorian was still staring at the door. Only the knowledge that bursting through would do more harm than good was keeping him from doing exactly that.

A squeeze on his shoulder again from Zac. "This is one fight we have to sit out. The girls have to do this one themselves. But I have no doubt they are both up for the challenge."

Zac and Finn didn't leave his side for the next hour. They reported security updates as they got them. Evidently Kendrick and Neo's grand plan was to have a huge influx of patients, who all happen to be related to Linear in some way, to further overwhelm the hospital computer system. That, combined with two celebrities—extreme sport sensation Riley "Phoenix" Harrison and country music singer Cade Conner—both coming in to be checked out for various ailments in the same night would make Ray's surgery merely one tiny aspect of a night that went crazy. Given how nurses were frantically running around everywhere, it looked like the plan was working.

When all their phones received a text at once, Dorian finally felt like he could breathe. It was from Girl Riley.

Out of surgery. Everyone okay. More details soon.

Dorian knew he wouldn't be able to truly relax until he saw Ray for himself, but this was a start. When Anne came out a few minutes later, she hugged him and kissed her husband, then seemed to understand Dorian's need to see Ray for himself. She led him down the hallway and into a room where Ray lay in a bed, unconscious, but breathing on her own. The IV hooked to her arm was the only thing that gave away the fact that she wasn't merely sleeping.

"Riley will stay with her. I need to talk to you in my office, if that's okay."

"Is she really all right, Anne?"

Anne nodded. "Yes. She's stupid because she had to have been in a huge amount of pain for the past few days and should've told someone, but she's going to be fine."

He'd been racking his brain about what could've been wrong with Ray. "Was it her appendix? Did it rupture or something?"

She touched him on the arm. "Let's get to my office and talk about it."

So it was complicated. That probably wasn't good news. But Ray was alive. Survival was always the most important thing.

Anne had changed into fresh surgical scrubs and led Dorian into her office, gesturing to one of the chairs as she sat down at her desk after pulling a bottle of water out of a small fridge.

"But she's really okay?"

"I promise. I assume you didn't know she was coming here tonight."

He rolled his eyes. "I know you ladies say that we men are too protective, but I think that goes both ways."

"Touché." Anne smiled at that. "When I told Ray the test results, she asked me if I believed in miracles. I'm going to ask you the same thing, Dorian, then I'll give you the whole story. Do you believe in miracles?"

He didn't hesitate. "Every day of my life. How could I not? I have Ray. I have Theo and Savannah. I have my mind, my mental health." That hadn't always been true. "All of them are miracles."

Anne's smile grew bigger. "Ray basically said the exact same thing. Well, let's add to the miracle list."

"Okay."

"Do you know what heterotopic pregnancy is?"

"No."

"Maybe you've heard of an ectopic pregnancy? A tubal pregnancy?"

Dorian nodded. He knew it wasn't good.

"I know Ray had her tubes tied years ago. But basically, a fertilized egg implanted in her fallopian tubes. Her tube ruptured tonight while she was here and we had to perform an emergency laparotomy, removing the remnant of the pregnancy and the fallopian tube itself. The gestational sac was pretty well developed, probably almost twelve weeks."

"Twelve weeks? What does that mean?"

Anne's features softened. "Mostly it means your wife is tough as hell. Any other woman probably would have come screaming to the doctor weeks ago because of the pain, but Ray just powered through."

Dorian scrubbed a hand down his face. "Of course she did. That's her MO. So, was this a miscarriage?"

"As I explained to her, the pregnancy was never viable.

There was never a chance of carrying it to term. But it's certainly appropriate to grieve the loss."

Dorian wasn't sure that he needed to grieve. "We have our kids, Anne. And they're more than we would've ever expected. So as long as Ray is going to be okay, that's all that matters."

Anne smiled again. "That's pretty much what Ray said too. But I—"

She stopped at a knock at the door. Zac stuck his head in. "Sorry to interrupt but we found a couple of concerned interlopers outside and thought you might want to talk to them yourself, Ghost."

Zac opened the door farther, revealing his kids' frightened faces. They rushed to him, and he immediately stood and dragged them in for a hug.

"Is Mom okay?" Savannah asked.

"She's fine. She had to have surgery, but she's resting now. Dr. Anne took good care of her." Savannah stayed attached to his waist but Theo took a step back. "How did you two get here? I left a note for you that I'd be back in the morning."

Theo shrugged. "We tracked your car on the computer, and when we saw you were at the hospital, we called Aunt Nadine to come and get us."

These two were way too fucking smart. Not only tracking him, but also calling Wyatt's wife, knowing she had the softest heart of the bunch and would do whatever they needed.

He narrowed his eyes at his son. "You shouldn't be tracking my vehicle on the computer."

Theo folded his arms in front of him, a gesture Dorian had to admit the kid had gotten from him. "Then you probably shouldn't have taught me how to do it."

The kid was thirteen and his son in every way that mattered. Dorian grinned and tussled his hair. "Smart ass."

He turned to Anne. "Can they stay in to hear the rest?"

"If that's okay with you. There's still more I need to tell you about Ray."

"Whatever it is, we'll weather it together." Savannah's little hand slipped into his. Theo stepped closer. Dorian looked at Zac. "You can stay too if you want. You're family."

Zac stepped closer to Anne and put a hand on her shoulder.

"If Ray hadn't been here tonight, if she'd been out at your cabin when her tube ruptured, she probably wouldn't have survived. Internal bleeding. The fact that she was inside the hospital when it happened was a miracle."

Dorian pulled his kids closer, his heart stopping for a second. "Told you I believed in miracles, Doc. And if I never get another my whole life, then tonight's will have been enough."

"I'm afraid that's not the only one you guys get. Ray's pregnancy was heterotopic. That means there was a nonviable pregnancy outside of the uterus. But what we discovered right before her fallopian tube ruptured was that Ray also has a viable intrauterine pregnancy."

Dorian's eyes left Anne's to look at Zac. Dorian didn't understand everything she was saying, but he understood the words *viable* and *pregnancy*. Zac shrugged, eyes wide.

"What? Are you saying— Do you mean—" Dorian felt a little dizzy. "I think I need to sit down."

Anne grinned. "It doesn't happen often after a tubal ligation, but it is possible. Ray is pregnant. This fetus looks to be about twelve weeks and seems to be fine."

Now he definitely needed to sit down. He collapsed into the chair.

Savannah's face crumpled. "Is Momma okay?"

Dorian pulled her onto his lap and wrapped his other arm around Theo.

"She's great," Anne told them. "You guys are going to be a big brother and sister. Because I have no doubt your family gets one more miracle."

Six months later, almost to the day, Amari Grace Lindstrom made her way into the world, mother and daughter both healthy.

Her name meant miracle.

Acknowledgments

SCOUT was originally part of the *Danger & Desire* multi-author box set, but because of the parameters of the collection, could only be a certainly length.

I'm so glad I was able to tell the full version of Wyatt and Nadine's story here. They deserved their happily-ever-after. They've waited a long time for it.

This book might contain my favorite line of all time: "a man who looks at me like I'm the reason God created rainbows." May we all find the person who looks at us that way.

Writing, as always, is a team effort. A special thanks to the team of alpha/beta readers, editors and proofers who make all the Linear Tactical books possible: Elizabeth, Susan, Marci, Dee, Marilize, Tesh, Aimee, Laurie. Thank you for keeping me from looking like a complete idiot. And doing it on a moment's notice.

Deranged Doctor Designs once again created a beautiful cover. I was concerned pink might look weird in a romantic suspense book. I was wrong. You were right. As always.

It's almost impossible to believe that the Linear Tactical series will end with the next book, BLAZE (although there will be a bonus Jess & Ethan book, with them all grown up). I appreciate that you have journeyed to Oak Creek with me for a dozen books. They've been a joy to write, I hope they've been just as much a joy to read. I promise to finish strong, and to make the next series (the Zodiac Tactical books) just as compelling.

Believe in heroes,

Janie

Also by Janie Crouch

LINEAR TACTICAL SERIES

Cyclone

Eagle

Shamrock

Angel

Ghost

Shadow

Echo

Phoenix

Baby

Storm

Redwood

Scout

Blaze

Forever

ZODIAC TACTICAL SERIES

Code Name: ARIES

INSTINCT SERIES (series complete)

Primal Instinct

Critical Instinct

Survival Instinct

THE RISK SERIES (series complete)

About the Author

"Passion that leaps right off the page." - Romantic Times Book Reviews

USA Today and Publishers Weekly bestselling author Janie Crouch writes what she loves to read: passionate romantic suspense featuring protective heroes. Her books have won multiple awards, including the National Readers Choice and Booksellers' Best.

After a six-year stint in Germany (due to her husband's job as support for the U.S. Military) Janie is back on U.S. soil and loves hanging out with her four almost-adult kids. Sometimes.

When she's not listening to the voices in her head—and even when she is—she enjoys engaging in all sorts of crazy adventures (200-mile relay races; Ironman Triathlons, treks to Mt. Everest Base Camp) traveling, and trying new recipes.

Her favorite quote: "Life is a daring adventure or nothing." ~ Helen Keller.

facebook.com/janiecrouch

amazon.com/author/janiecrouch

instagram.com/janiecrouch

bookbub.com/authors/janie-crouch

Made in the USA
Monee, IL
05 March 2021